Praise for the woks

An Acquired Taste

An Acquired Taste is very cute! I appreciated how sweet the romance is and I enjoyed spending time with these characters and watching them fall in love.

-*The Lesbian Review*

This is the first time I've read a book by Cheri Ritz, and I wasn't disappointed. ...This book was cute, with some funny moments. I found once started, it was difficult to put down, 'Just one more chapter' comes to mind.

-Cathy W., *NetGalley*

...Ms. Ritz has brought together two women that you will find yourself rooting for. Great characters and great supporting cast has made this a very entertaining read. Very, very good.

-Bonnie S., *NetGalley*

...The cooking in the book made me itch to start prepping, creating, cooking and eating. The visuals you get in your mind's eyes while Elle brought Ashley on a culinary learning journey were such a plus that you can literally smell and taste the food and of them falling in love. I thoroughly enjoyed the read as the book has the same satisfying end akin to a good meal that leaves you feeling upbeat, wholesome and all around happy.

-Nutmeg, *NetGalley*

Vacation People

The character work is solid, the relationship is developed well, and the settings seemed vivid. If you like vacation romances, you should pick up *Vacation People*. I'm looking forward to seeing more stories from Cheri Ritz in the future, because this was a great debut.

-*The Lesbian Review*

Under New Management

Cheri Ritz

Other Bella Books By Cheri Ritz

Vacation People
Let the Beat Drop
Love's No Joke
Low Key Love
An Acquired Taste

About The Author

Cheri Ritz is a Pittsburgh native, wife, mom of 3, and author of several books published with Bella Books. She loves reading romance novels, so writing happily ever afters is a dream come true for her. She enjoys binge watching her favorite TV shows, crafting, and 80's and 90's pop culture. You can catch her around Pittsburgh trying new IPAs, hanging at home with her wife and sons, or working on her next novel.

Under
New
Management

Cheri Ritz

BELLA
BOOKS

2024

Bella Books, Inc.
P.O. Box 10543
Tallahassee, FL 32302

First Edition - 2024

Editor: Cath Walker

ISBN: 978-1-64247-569-2

PUBLISHER'S NOTE

Acknowledgments

Thank you to Jessica and Linda Hill, and all the fine folks at Bella Books. I appreciate all you do to put these stories out into the world. Thank you also to my editor, Cath Walker. This story would not be what it is today without your excellent guidance.

I have some awesome writer pals who help me along in this journey—I'm looking at you, Writer Roundtable group! A special shout-out to my dear friend Brooke Campbell for the writing sprints/gab sessions that help shape words into full stories. A big thank you also to Gina Moser for sharing insights on contracts and law and helping me to sort all those technical bits and to Julia Heflin for the marketing assistance.

I couldn't do this without the support of my family. Jaime and my boys—hugs and kisses of thanks to all of you.

Finally, thank you so much to the readers. Whether you took a first-time-read chance on my book, or you came back for more, I love sharing my stories with you and I appreciate you.

For my wife. Bellissima!

CHAPTER ONE

Gabriella D'Angelo woke bright and early Sunday morning knowing that this was the day she'd been waiting years for. Today was *the* day.

Which made it especially disheartening that her whole body seemed to be staging a revolt. The headache she could easily attribute to one too many beers, but the strain in her shoulders and the tightness in her thighs, that could only be…She turned her head and peeped out of one eye to assess the situation. Yep. The beautiful blonde she had picked up at the bar was still slumbering peacefully in the bed beside her.

Oh, yes. At least last night's beer hadn't robbed her of the memory of what had transpired after they'd caught a ride back to the house. The way Blondie bit and nipped in all the right places as she had explored Gabi's body…yes, indeed. The way the woman screamed with pleasure when Gabi had brought her to orgasm was well worth a few aches and pains. Hell, a sore body the next day was how you knew it was good. It had been way too long since the last time Gabi had had a night like that.

The blonde—what was her name?—expelled a sleepy sigh and rolled onto her side. The sheet tugged down with the movement, exposing her perky breasts. Gabi's insides revved up all over again. Another orgasm could definitely chase away this hangover headache. Was there time for another round before she had to be at work?

A quick glance at her phone confirmed there was not. Gabi couldn't be late today—not when they were shutting the restaurant down after lunch service to prepare for the big party that evening.

Oh well, it had been good while it lasted. Time to cut this one loose.

It wasn't that the woman lying next to her wasn't totally fun and perfectly sexy, it was just that Gabi was on the precipice of a long-awaited change. Her father was retiring and she was taking over the family business. D'Angelo's Italian Restaurant was a popular feature of the community. She needed to focus. She couldn't let her family—not to mention the community—down. She didn't need the distraction of maintaining a relationship. So, no. This was the end, not the beginning of anything. One-and-dones were all it was going to be for Gabi in the romance department.

But right now the beautiful woman was gently snoring and slumbering sweetly, and there was no reason Gabi couldn't wait until after she was dressed to wake…Ashley? Audrey? Whatever her name was. She covered those beautiful breasts back up before slipping out of bed.

By the time she returned from the shower, her sleepover guest was yawning and stretching awake, blinking hard as if trying to fit all the pieces of last night together into a full memory. Relatable.

"Hey there," Gabi said, pulling on a plain gray, long-sleeve tee. "I don't want to rush you out, but I've got to get to work, so, uh—"

"So, you're rushing me out," she finished. Her easy laugh was like a babbling brook. Damn, she had a stunning smile. She didn't seem at all thrown by the nudge to hit the road. Instead, she leaned over the side of the bed to retrieve her clothes from the floor. "It's all right. I understand."

It was only a moment before they were both fully dressed and heading down the stairs. At the front door, Gabi turned to face the other woman. "This is kind of awkward, right?"

"Oh, no. It's fine." That smile again. It was vanilla-latte warm and sweet. "Last night was fun. I'm Ainsley, by the way."

"Gabi." She shook the offered hand, relieved that their parting was so easy-peasy. "Do you need me to order a car for you or something?"

"I think I'm going to walk. I'm just a few blocks away. I'm staying at the Hilton." She tipped her head, indicating she was going north. Her expression clouded for a moment as if she was trying to solve a difficult math problem, but then she shook her head and brightened again. "Anyway, I'm gonna run. See you around."

Gabi said goodbye, turned, and walked in the other direction. That went well. The least sticky one-night-stand morning-after she'd ever experienced. Not that she had had a ton of them, but enough since her last disaster of a relationship ended and she had decided to throw herself into work.

This had been an easy catch and release. Smooth as silk. Completely unsticky. In a way it made the woman even more attractive. Golden hair, big blue sparkle-like-the-sun-on-the-ocean eyes, that sexy mouth and the very, very dirty things it did to her, and on top of it all, an easy breezy demeanor that left one wondering what it would be like if…

It didn't matter—it was over and Gabi had to get to work. She had to get ready for lunch service and pull together the last-minute bits and pieces for the party later that night.

Maybe she would run into Ainsley again sometime and they could spend another nice and easy night together. Gabi inhaled the brisk spring morning air. What was that perfume of Ainsley's? Some kind of cherry blossom scent. Her heart felt lighter somehow. Yes. Running into Ainsley again wouldn't be completely objectionable.

* * *

"It's a beautiful day to make marinara!" Gabi was still flying high fifteen minutes later when she walked through the back door into the kitchen of D'Angelo's Italian Restaurant. "What's the good word, Brian?"

"The good word?" Brian's deep voice held a teasing tone. "Someone's in a good mood. Something happened last night that you want to share with the class?"

Brian had been working at D'Angelo's since he was a teenager, hired as a dishwasher and to unload the truck. Now, at twenty-five and built like a linebacker, he still helped with the truck, but was also Gabi's right-hand man in the kitchen and the only one Gabi trusted to run it on her days off. His square jaw and meaty hands gave him a grizzly look, but Gabi knew him well enough to know he was all teddy bear inside. In the four years since she'd come back to town and they'd been working together, they'd become more like family than just coworkers. Still, Gabi wasn't exactly ready to confess about her hot and heavy one-night stand, as amazing as it had been.

"I'm just excited about the party tonight."

"Really?" He wiped his hands on the towel hanging through the belt loop on his well-worn jeans and stepped around the steel prep table, coming closer as if trying to get a better look at her. "Because you're practically glowing. If I didn't know better, I'd think maybe you got—"

"I said I'm just excited about tonight." She pushed into his beefy shoulder, intending to shove him back in the direction he came from, but he didn't even flinch. "The party is going to be a blast."

"And let's not forget, the announcement that you're taking over D'Angelo's now that your dad is retiring." His teasing expression turned more sincere, like he was proud of her.

"There's that too." Gabi couldn't help the huge smile that took over her face. She'd been waiting a long time. Not the part about her pop retiring—she loved working with him. But the next generation taking over the family restaurant, that was tradition. And now it was finally her turn.

"Hey, you two," her father called through the back door, interrupting Gabi's moment of blissful reflection. "Get out here. The truck just pulled up and he can't block the ally all day while he waits for you two to swap secrets in the kitchen."

Brian shrugged. "He's still the one in charge today."

The two did as they were told, grabbing a dolly on the way out to assist with transferring produce and supplies from the truck to the walk-in cooler.

Gabi helped for a bit, but after the bulk of the order had been unloaded, she began her lunch prep in the kitchen and left Brian and her father to inventory the supplies. She'd barely finished prepping for the day's featured chopped salad before a string of cursing came from the walk-in that made her think she'd better check in on the guys.

"Pop, what's wrong?" She leaned against the cold, metal door and looked from her father, digging through a crate of tomatoes, to Brian, holding a printed copy of the order in one hand and scratching at one of his bushy eyebrows with the other.

"These aren't Roma tomatoes. My standing order is Roma. These are…"

"Saucy lady tomatoes," Brian supplied.

"Saucy lady? What kind of name is that for a tomato?" He dropped the fruit back into the case and threw his hands in the air as if appealing to the gods.

"I don't know, Pop. It sounds pretty descriptive to me."

"It's not a Roma." His voice was loud. This wasn't a joke to him. "I order Romas because that's what we use in my nonna's sauce. I need the Romas. Not saucy ladies or whatever they're called. Do these jagoffs think they can just send whatever they want and no one will notice?"

"What's it say on the packing slip?" Gabi turned to Brian.

He squinted at the paper and worked his brow a little more, nervous about possibly upsetting his boss. "Roma is crossed out on the list." More rubbing. He was going to rub that thing right off at this rate. "But three cases of saucy lady tomatoes have been added at the end. Guess they swapped them out?"

"How the hell am I supposed to make my sauce without Romas?"

"God, Pop. If I hear you say Romas one more time, I'm going to scream." She put her arm around her father and guided him out of the walk-in, leaving Brian to sort the rest of the order. "Why don't we call the supplier and ask if this is just a mix-up. I'm sure if it is they'll make it right."

She would have preferred to send an email, but she couldn't listen to her pop stomp around the kitchen muttering about tomatoes for the rest of the morning while she waited for a response. So she pulled him away from the noise of the kitchen into his office—the office that would be her office in less than twenty-four hours—and made the call. While the tinny hold music played in her ear and her father paced in the small office, she let her mind drift.

The office was the one part of the restaurant that hadn't been renovated since her father took over operations in 1993. The dining room got a refresh in 2015. The kitchen got an overhaul a few years after that. But this space? Nothing. This should be her first order of business once she was officially in charge. A fresh coat of paint—maybe a bolder color choice than the mint green currently chipping away on the wall. Definitely a new desk chair. This one looked like it had survived the Nixon administration and had a wobbly wheel that was a safety hazard. She could give this tiny space some style and really make it her own.

"Thank you for holding. How can I help you?" The woman on the other end of the call drew Gabi's focus back to the matter at hand and was quickly able to explain how the Great Tomato Swap had gone down.

Gabi clicked off the call and pulled up a file on the office laptop. Yep. Just like the nice lady at Laberto Brothers Foods had said. "Pop, did you even read this contract you have with Labertos?"

He put his hands on her shoulders and peered at the screen. "What's to read? I tell them what I need, they bring it. So long as I get my food, it's all good."

"Right." She blew out an exasperated sigh. How on Earth had her father kept this place afloat all these years without caring about anything but the food? Good thing he had her—and a great staff—for support. "See this little box here labeled *no substitutions* that you didn't tick? That means if they don't have the exact item you requested, but *do* have a reasonable substitution, they will make the replacement. Thus, the saucy ladies."

Her pop growled, "But our sauce—"

"Is going to feature seventy-five pounds of saucy lady tomatoes this week." She cut off his complaining. "People will get over it. By the weekend we'll be back to Roma and the ship will be righted."

"With the wrong tomatoes?"

"We're not wasting the food or losing the money we paid for them. So, go make friends with the saucy lady, Pop."

He growled again, but based on the way he shuffled back out to the kitchen, seemed to surrender to Gabi's declaration.

That was that. *Success!* Gabi had officially made her first executive decision as manager of D'Angelo's. No doubt the first of many to come. She was more than ready, and she was totally going to rock her new gig running the family business.

* * *

Her father was about to announce he was retiring and handing his restaurant over to her good care. But instead of enjoying the party leading up to her big moment, she was ducking into the bathroom to wipe onion dip off her chest.

She turned on the cold tap, splashed some water onto the stain, and dabbed at it with a cocktail napkin. She frowned when she saw the baseball-sized wet spot in the mirror. The clingy damp green fabric didn't make her feel any better.

"Just call me onion tits," she muttered then jumped when a toilet flushed and a stall door slammed open behind her.

"I'm sorry, were you talking to me?" The tall blonde was striking even in her plain white button-down and straight-cut black pants and Gabi recognized her right away—Ainsley the unsticky one-night stand. Was she one of the servers they'd hired for the evening so the staff could enjoy the party? That was a little embarrassing. Recognition registered on Ainsley's face. "Oh hi. Gabi, right?"

"Yeah. And no, I was just talking to myself. Sorry. I...I spilled dip on my shirt, and I tried to clean it off, and now my shirt's all wet." Thank you, Catherine Obvious. Why was she oversharing? Ainsley didn't seem to mind. She was drying her hands under the air dryer and going on with her life. "Anyway, I'm fine."

"Maybe you should put your shirt under here." Her voice was still friendly even though she was speaking loudly enough to be heard over the blowing air. She backed away from the device and tipped her head in an invitation for Gabi to step up to the hot blast.

As much as she twisted and bent backward limbo-style, Gabi just couldn't quite get her breast positioned under the flow of air. This was never going to work.

Ainsley was trying to stifle her laughter with a perfectly manicured hand pressed against her lips. "I'm sorry." She shook her head and at least had the decency to look like she was trying to bite back her mirth. She gestured with a flapping hand. "Gimme your shirt."

"Give you what?" Gabi straightened her posture. Was she kidding? She wanted her to strip down to her bra right there in the restroom?

"Take your shirt off and give it to me. Come on. I've done this before," she said. Her friendly voice now had a confident and commanding edge. Bossy. Sexy. "We'll get you dried out and back to the party in no time."

Outside the bathroom the music pumping through the speakers stopped and Gabi heard her pop thanking everyone for coming to the party. Maybe it was desperation to not miss his speech, or maybe it was those big, blue eyes staring her down, daring her to defy the order, but Gabi pulled her top over her head and handed it over. She stood there in her bra, arms crossed self-consciously over her chest, and rocked on her heels while Ainsley swiftly slid the shirt back and forth under the blast of hot air.

"Perfect!" Ainsley was suddenly facing her.

Was she talking about Gabi's boobs? *No.* She was holding up the green top which looked good as new.

"Oh my God." Gabi grabbed the top and pulled it on. "Thank you so much. I really appreciate this."

"Happy to help." Ainsley smiled. "Now, go on. Go. It sounds like Mr. D'Angelo is about to give a speech."

Gabi did as she was instructed, making it back to the party just in time. Her pop caught her eye and his face lit up.

"There she is." His voice boomed through the speaker system. "Get up here, Gabriella. Friends, I'm so proud to announce that my daughter, Gabriella, will be filling my spot in the D'Angelo's kitchen. She will be the head chef guaranteeing you will continue to get the same delicious food just like you've always loved here."

Gabi reached her father's side and waved at the crowd applauding her. She had some big shoes to fill, but she was ready for the challenge. And it felt so good to have the support of the family and friends who had gathered to celebrate with them. Finally, it was her moment, and it felt glorious.

"Happy day for this proud papa," he continued, pulling Gabi to him in a side hug. "I also want to take this chance to introduce you all to D'Angelo's new front-of-house business manager, Ainsley Becker. Ainsley, you come on up here too so everyone can see who you are."

Wait, what? Gabi's knees felt like cooked spaghetti. She wasn't taking over the business in its entirety? Her dad was bringing in some stranger to manage the general operations? She saw the tall blonde working her way through the partygoers to join them in front of the crowd and her stomach dropped.

Ainsley was wearing what looked like a bespoke fitted violet jacket over the plain white button-down Gabi had seen when she was standing half-naked in the ladies' room two minutes earlier. The same friendly, bossy, sexy woman who helped Gabi dry her shirt and had given her more than a few mind-blowing orgasms the night before was now standing beside her and waving to the crowd like she was fucking Miss America. And apparently she was taking over half of Gabi's family business.

What the fuck?

CHAPTER TWO

Ainsley Becker spent the short ride from D'Angelo's to her new temporary housing trying to figure out why Gabriella—with whom she'd spent a pretty damn good night less than twenty-four hours ago and whom she'd completely saved from a fate of being labeled "onion tits"—spent the last hour of the party scowling at her.

Part of Gustare Foods' contract with Bruno D'Angelo included keeping his daughter, Gabriella, on as kitchen manager during the transition. Ainsley had expected that meant she'd be grateful to be part of the team, not glare and pout like a petulant child. Either way, she hadn't put together that the "Gabi" she'd met upon her arrival in Pittsburgh was *that* Gabriella. She was still kicking herself for that. Her employer, one hundred percent, frowned upon sleeping with the client.

Too bad. She'd had a good time with Gabi the night before. It wasn't just the sex either. Gabi was funny and vibrant. It was Gabi's life-of-the-party demeanor at the bar that had attracted her in the first place. And she was a homeowner! Very adult.

They'd taken a rideshare from the bar to Gabi's house. It was a simple, skinny two-story place, similar to the others on the block, and though the décor was sparse, the space was neat and clean. And, best of all, she lived alone—no roommates—which was a relief since they were pretty enthusiastically going at it from the very second they'd closed the front door behind them. Yes, it had been a very good night.

She was pulled out of her reverie as the car arrived at her destination. She looked up at the yellow-shingled house where she would be living during her stay in Bloomfield and wondered which of the windows would be part of her quarters. She'd come into town two days earlier but had been staying at the Hilton until her lease started. She'd intended to move into the house before the party at D'Angelo's, but after her all-nighter with Gabi, she'd taken a nap in her hotel room that lasted a little too long. She'd ended up just taking her belongings with her to the restaurant and leaving a message for her new landlord that her arrival would be delayed. At seven o'clock Sunday evening she was finally there.

"Hello!" a chirpy voice called from the stoop of the three-story house in front of her. "Can I give you a hand with those?"

Ainsley boosted her duffel bag on her shoulder and picked her suitcases up off the sidewalk. She'd been standing there under the streetlamp, lost in her thoughts since her ride had dropped her off. "No, thanks. I've got them."

"I'm assuming you're Ainsley. I'm Ruby Truman. You're lucky. Every year Pittsburgh gets one unnaturally warm weekend near the end of March. You caught the tail end of it. But don't be fooled, spring is not really here yet. In a couple days we'll be back to the cool weather." The chirpy voice didn't match the short, squat body wearing a hot-pink housecoat and matching rubber-soled slippers, but it was welcoming. She propped the storm door open with her butt and seemed to size Ainsley up as she entered, her gaze lingering on the Louis Vuitton luggage she was dragging in with her. "I hope you'll be comfortable here, dear. I know it's not fancy, but it's home."

Once inside the front door, Ainsley surveyed her surroundings. A small table in the entryway was draped with lace doilies, the powder-blue shag carpeting was worn bare in some spots, and a wallpaper frieze featuring white geese wearing colorful bows around their long necks adorned the walls of the hallway. No, fancy wasn't exactly the word for it.

Ainsley had been quite pleased to find rental accommodation less than a mile from the restaurant. If she hadn't had her luggage with her, she would have enjoyed the walk. Ruby seemed like she might be a bit of an acquired taste, and her home may not have been redecorated since the mideighties, but the elderly woman was friendly, and the place was clean. She assumed her side of the duplex home would be as well. And since Ruby had been agreeable to renting to her month-to-month, Ainsley was feeling pretty good about her Gustare Foods assignment in Bloomfield—a place her boss had assured her was a charming Pittsburgh neighborhood.

"Come on, honey." Ruby took one of the suitcases and waddled toward a staircase at the end of the hall. "I'll show you your side of the place."

Ainsley followed, their slow pace up the steps giving her ample time to inspect the cluster of framed photographs of smiling, happy people on various special occasions. Ainsley's mother had never hung photos in any of their houses when she was growing up, only art. She recognized a younger Ruby in some of the photos, and she assumed the others were family members. "How long have you lived here?"

"Oh, I've been in this house almost forty-five years," Ruby replied over her shoulder and seemed to notice Ainsley studying the photos. "Oh, those were taken at the Slice of Italy Festival over the years. Anyway, I've lived in Bloomfield my whole life."

"So, you love it here then." Ainsley smiled when she noticed the rotary phone perched on a little wooden table at the top of the stairs. Ruby was a real blast from the past.

"Family all lived here. Friends all lived here. What's not to love?" Ruby shrugged. The climb seemed to limit her chattering.

At the top of the stairs, she dipped her gray head to fiddle with a set of keys, presumably looking for the correct one. "This one is yours." She handed the key over.

Ainsley pushed through the door and was pleasantly surprised by the size of the space. High ceilings and loads of natural light in the living room area thanks to the two large street-facing windows. A small kitchen area that would suit her needs. Another doorway led to her bedroom with a tall handsome wardrobe, and a dresser that would provide more storage than she could possibly fill. The eyelet bedspread tracked with Ruby's interior design sensibilities, but at least there weren't doilies everywhere. The valences adorning the windows left a little to be desired, but...

"Why don't you go ahead and settle in. I'll be down in my kitchen making some tea and setting out some cookies if you want to join me. I like a little snack before bed. Sets you up for sweet dreams. I'll leave my door cracked. Just come on in," Ruby said before finally leaving Ainsley alone in the room.

She set to work filling the dresser, but it didn't take very long. At this point in her life she didn't even own much more than the things she'd brought along with her. She had a few boxes stored in her parents' place in Florida, but that was it.

This was only Ainsley's second assignment with Gustare Foods and she'd learned a valuable lesson about signing a yearlong apartment lease when her mission was for an indeterminate amount of time. The last restaurant job only took three months soup to nuts, then she was instructed to relocate to Pittsburgh. She had to break her lease in that little town outside of Buffalo, and that meant losing a sizable chunk of change. This time she'd specifically searched out a month-to-month rental. Ruby's place fit the bill. Who knew how long the assignment at D'Angelo's would take. Hopefully, just three months, but based on the hard stare Gabriella had fixed on her after the old man's announcement, it could take some time to get things at the restaurant shipshape and running smoothly.

And based on the way Gabriella looked standing in the restroom in nothing but her bra, and the way they'd gotten along the previous night, maybe Ainsley wouldn't totally mind.

"Tea's ready," Ruby called out from downstairs, pulling Ainsley's thoughts back to the present. A little something sweet sounded good, plus it wouldn't hurt to get to know the woman she'd be sharing the house with.

* * *

Ainsley's stomach grumbled with anticipation when she saw the plate of cookies Ruby had set out on the square Formica kitchen table. There had been plenty of food at the party, but she'd abstained on the grounds of appearing professional, and mostly to avoid a mishap like onion dip on her blouse à la Gabriella D'Angelo.

She'd felt stunned when she discovered her one-night stand in the bathroom at her new assignment. That low, sultry voice had set her heart racing even before she'd actually put eyes on the woman. She'd opened the stall door and saw those springing curls of chocolate-brown hair, and her chest hummed with hope. Then her gaze met Gabi's enchanting dark-brown eyes in the mirror, and a shiver of excitement had raced up her spine. What were the chances that they would run into each other again so soon after their scorching hot encounter? Apparently, the beautiful Gabriella hadn't been expecting her either. Sure, it was a shock, but her hostile attitude seemed unreasonable.

Ainsley was a professional; she would make it all work out somehow. Anyway, now seemed like the perfect time to enjoy a chocolate chip cookie and maybe one of the little cream-filled flaky things on the plate. She wasn't wrong—the first sugary bite was so heavenly, she moaned.

"Ah, the lady locks are my favorites too," Ruby said as she brought two steaming mugs of tea to the table and sat down across from her. "They're a Pittsburgh wedding cookie table staple, but I say they're perfect any time."

"Wedding cookie table?" An image of furniture fashioned out of gingerbread flashed in Ainsley's mind. "That sounds very Hansel and Gretel."

"It's nothing like that, dear." Ruby laughed. "Having a table filled with cookies at a wedding is a Pittsburgh tradition. Some couples even provide guests with baggies to fill to take home. Like a party favor, only tastier. Of course, if they don't provide baggies, a napkin stashed in your purse will do the trick. You've never seen that at a wedding before?"

Ainsley shook her head and popped the last bite of the lady lock into her mouth.

Ruby squeezed a wedge of lemon into her tea. "You're not from around here I suppose."

"No, I'm from..." Ainsley paused and blew across the surface of her hot tea. "I'm not from here. I lived in Chitaqua, New York during my last assignment with Gustare Foods. Well, it was actually my first assignment with Gustare Foods. This is only my second.

"You're new to the business then?"

"Not new to the company," Ainsley said between sips of tea. "Just the position. I've worked at headquarters for just about three years developing procedures and controls. I've been promoted, and now my job is out in the field putting those procedures into action for restaurants that need a little assistance getting business back on track."

"So that's what you're doing over there at D'Angelo's? Getting them back on track?" Ruby raised a curious eyebrow. "Are they in some kind of financial trouble or something?"

Ainsley took a bite of a chocolate chip cookie and chewed slowly. Stalling.

Ruby's question might just be general curiosity, or it could be an attempt to poke around for some neighborhood scuttlebutt. Either way Ainsley was tiptoeing on the edge of disclosing company information she should be holding close to the vest. Ruby had been very sweet since her arrival, and she seemed like a nice little old lady. But Ainsley had to remember she wasn't in town to make friends; she was there to do a job. And doing that job meant not blabbing confidential client information.

She tried to fix her face into a friendly smile and brushed the crumbs from her lips before she answered, "No, no trouble. Just helping Mr. D'Angelo smooth the transition into retirement."

"Ah, well Gabi's going to do a great job running the place." Ruby nodded and plucked a peanut butter blossom from the plate. "Such a nice girl."

"Mmmm," Ainsley murmured noncommittally. She wasn't entirely sure how well Ruby knew Gabriella, but she didn't want to ask any questions that may lead to a full-blown discussion about her. As far as Ainsley was concerned, the jury was still out. Sure, Gabriella had seemed quite something the night before, and they'd shared a giggle in the bathroom earlier, but for the rest of the evening she'd actually been downright cold. Those once flirty, pretty brown eyes had done nothing but give her the hard stare after Mr. D'Angelo announced Ainsley would be managing the dining room at the restaurant for the time being. The change had been enough to give a girl whiplash. She replied with a neutral, "I'm sure we'll work well together."

Ruby reached across the table and covered Ainsley's hand with her own, as if she sensed she could use the comforting touch and boost to her confidence. "I bet the two of you will get along famously."

She wasn't exactly sure about that, but it was her job to make it happen, so she would. It was strictly business, and she didn't need to be best friends with Gabriella D'Angelo to get the job done.

CHAPTER THREE

It was a few minutes before seven on Monday morning when Gabi arrived at D'Angelo's. She always got an early start on food prep on Mondays, but this particular morning she wanted to get to the restaurant before her father made an appearance. And even though he had officially retired, she had no doubt he would be in when her Uncle Sal made his weekly wine delivery. For the past twenty-five years the two D'Angelo brothers had breakfast together after the delivery. There was no way a little thing like retirement was going to stop that.

The stockpots full of tomato sauce and D'Angelo's special combination of seasonings weren't the only things simmering as Gabi went through her morning prep routine. As she chopped and sliced onions, peppers, and various other vegetables, anger and hurt were still bubbling just under the surface. The plan had always been for her to take over managing the restaurant when her father retired. At least *she* thought that was the plan. When had it changed for him?

She got into a rhythm prepping salad ingredients, then roasting heads of garlic and making the butter for D'Angelo's signature garlic bread, but her thoughts continued to swirl. *Focus dammit!* Losing concentration in the kitchen could lead to dangerous mistakes. She needed to take the morning task by task and pay attention to what she was doing. Mentally playing out conversations with her father wouldn't get the kitchen ready to open any faster, nor would it do anything for her mood. Soon staff would start rolling in and she couldn't let them see her flustered. She still had a kitchen to run.

"There's my beautiful daughter!" her father boomed as he came through the back entrance to the kitchen just a little after nine o'clock. Just as expected. "Hell of a party last night, huh?"

Gabi took a deep breath to center herself. "Hey, Pop."

She deliberately took her time checking the pots of sauce on the stove. She lifted the lid off one and gave it a stir before doing the same with the second. A warm burst of the delicious aroma filled her senses. The sauce would be ready when her workstation smelled like her nonna's kitchen—the perfect amount of garlic with a touch of oregano and basil, all graced with a little sweetness. A sauce recipe handed down through four generations of her father's family. A sauce recipe beloved by their customers. A sauce recipe Gabi was damn proud of, just like she was about everything at her family's restaurant.

She glanced over at her pop just in time to see him disappear down the steps to the wine cellar. Waxing poetically about marinara wasn't going to get her the answers she needed. She needed to face her pop and speak the words that had been tumbling around in her mind since the party the night before.

"Hey, Brian, keep an eye on things for a minute. I'm gonna help Pop with the wine," she called over her shoulder, wiping her hands on her apron and heading for the stairs.

At the bottom she found he had propped the door to the wine cellar open to keep the broken latch from catching. She would need to add it on her list of things to handle as kitchen manager. Or, better yet, fuck it. Let Ainsley Becker handle it.

She found her father already at work rotating stock, humming away. She couldn't recall him ever humming while working before. Already retirement seemed to be suiting him, despite the fact that he was kind of still working. She fell into rhythm with him grabbing a couple of bottles and moving them to the crate by the stairs to be transferred up to the bar.

"Don't you have a kitchen to run?" He smiled kindly at her—the smile that had always made things better when she was a little kid. Bruno D'Angelo wasn't a big man—at five foot eight he was only a couple of inches taller than Gabi, but he carried himself with a king's confidence. His demeanor demanded respect, and rarely did anyone deny him that. Underneath that rough exterior though he was really a big softy. Especially when it came to family.

"Yeah, Pop. About that…"

He stopped rearranging bottles and turned his full attention to her, the cringe around his eyes indicating he suspected what was coming. "Aw, sweetheart, don't get angry with your old man."

"It's too late for that, Pop. I'm angry already. What are you bringing some outsider in for when I'm perfectly capable of managing the place? I thought that was the plan—you retire and I take over for you. Managing D'Angelo's."

"You *are* managing D'Angelo's. You're in charge of the kitchen, the heart of the whole place. You're the boss, kiddo."

"Pop." She hated how whiny her voice sounded, but she was running out of patience, plus if Uncle Sal got there with the wine before they finished the conversation, it would be dropped and she'd have to work up the steam to confront him all over again. "Come on."

He sighed and put a gentle hand on her shoulder. "Gabriella, you are an excellent chef and you run the kitchen like nobody else. But the front of house—it's just not your strong point. So, I brought in a consultant."

"This Becker woman is some kind of consultant?"

"She works for a company that comes in and does this kind of thing. They offer support to family-run restaurants to keep them running smoothly when they're going through a transition." He sounded like he was quoting a brochure. "Joey's nephew over at Russo's in the North Hills hired them when he took over the business at the end of last year. It seemed to work for them."

"She works for some company? Pop, what did you do?"

"I made sure D'Angelo's was going to continue on here in the neighborhood, that's what." He went back to organizing the wine bottles. "And I don't appreciate you second-guessing my decision. I'm your father, I know what's best. I ran this restaurant for years."

"I know you did, but I could've taken it over on my own. All of it. I thought that's what we always talked about."

"That's what *you* always talked about." He grimaced. Whether it was from all the bending and lifting, or from what he had to say next was unclear. "You can't run the front of house. Not yet. You have a tendency to lose your temper. You boss people around and shout and swear. That's fine back in the kitchen where guests can't see or hear you. It works back here. But you can't do it out front. Managing the front requires a little more…finesse."

"I've never done that to the front-of-house staff."

"But you have lost your temper in the dining room."

Gabi's cheeks burned with embarrassment. He didn't need to say anything more for her to know exactly to what he was referring. Neither of them really wanted to revisit that incident anyway. It was too damn humiliating.

"So, you brought in *some company* to help?"

"When Joey Russo's nephew took over running things for him, the kid was a mess, but Gustare Foods came in and got Russo's running smooth as silk. Streamlined everything, the kid said."

"And you think I'm a mess too?" What a punch in the gut. Gabi had worked her ass off for years trying to prove herself to her father. Didn't any of that matter? "A mess like Joey Russo's nephew?"

"Not at all, kiddo." He shook his head. "I just want to give D'Angelo's the best chance possible to carry on. This is our family business. Our family name. Our restaurant has been a part of Bloomfield for over fifty years. It's my legacy. Can you understand that—what it means to me? Can't you just give this a try for your old man?"

She understood. Family was what D'Angelo's was all about—what it had always been about. Her grandfather had started the restaurant based on a love of the food and the recipes his mother had taught him. No outside company would ever understand that. Her father took over when her grandfather passed away and taught her to love cooking too. Gabi was the one who knew the place inside and out. No stranger could come in and just know what was best for her family's business.

Still, the restaurant was her grandfather's dream and apparently her pop's legacy for their community. The two of them had been a team for a long time. She at least owed him the chance to do it his way. That didn't mean she had to like Ainsley Becker, or even make things easy on her. Gabi would do her best to move Ainsley and her consulting company right back out the door as soon as possible. She just needed to let their time there run its—hopefully short—course.

"Okay, Pop. You win," she acquiesced. "We'll do it your way."

Before her father could say anything else, footsteps creaking down the old, wooden staircase announced Uncle Sal. "I've got the vino!" His robust tone matched her father's usual cheerful boom. Just one of the many things the brothers had in common, like their receding hairlines and their love of Pittsburgh football. "You gonna help or what? Don't tell me retirement's already made you into a lazy jagoff."

While the men went up to bring in the new stock, Gabi grabbed a few bottles to cover the upcoming lunch rush. Time to get back to it now that she had a plan. She would be patient and manage the kitchen until Ainsley cleared out. Then she'd have her day to truly head up D'Angelo's and make her pop proud.

* * *

"Happy Monday," Danielle greeted her from behind the bar where she was busy stocking clean glasses. "What's with the frown?"

Gabi deposited the wine onto the bar then slumped onto it herself. "What's with the happy?"

"C'mon, Gabs. It's not so bad."

Of course, it wasn't so bad for Danielle. Her job would remain the same. In addition to being Gabi's best friend, Danielle was the daytime bartender at D'Angelo's. Because the bar wasn't exactly hopping from ten to five, she also waited tables. That wouldn't change with the arrival of Ainsley Becker, sexy one-night stand and professional know-it-all. Danielle's job was steady, and she would be doing what she thought she would be doing. Not like Gabi who'd been sidelined. "I shouldn't complain, at least I can hide out in the kitchen and not have to interact with the corporate stooge boss lady."

"Gabi—"

"No." Gabi popped back up and slapped her hands on the bar. "You can't tell me you're not the least bit upset about some total stranger blowing into town and telling me and you—who have been working here since we were teenagers—how to do our jobs. Seriously, what do we need some Business Management Barbie changing things around here for?"

Instead of answering the question, or commiserating with a snarky pile on, Danielle pressed her lips into a straight line and flicked her gaze over Gabi's shoulder.

"You think I look like Barbie? I'm going to go ahead and take that as a compliment. Because, you know, Barbie can do anything. She's a total badass."

Gabi didn't need to turn around to know it was Ainsley's voice right behind her. She tried to stop cringing before swiveling to face her. "I didn't mean that you…all I'm saying is that…" *Crap.* She was busted. There were no two ways about it. "Is there any chance you only caught that last little bit?"

"Oh, I caught the whole corporate stooge inspired thing." Based on how Ainsley's eyebrow hitched up, she was not amused. "Danielle, I'd like to show you the revised bar inventory checklist and review the new processes with you this morning before the servers' meeting."

"Wow, you're diving right in, eh?" For a minute, Gabi had almost felt bad for what she'd said. But now that she was witnessing firsthand how Ainsley was pushing her Gustare Foods agenda on Danielle without even the pretense of easing into it, she decided the judgment was totally deserved. "Okay, whatever. I've got to get back to the kitchen. I'll talk to you later, Danielle." She paused for a moment before pushing past Ainsley and giving her a stiff nod. "Barbie."

Back in the safety of her kitchen, Gabi settled into her food-prep routine. She still had to make the meat mixture for stuffing the peppers as well as the green pepper soup dinner special, along with the regular items she made every day.

An hour and a half later, she had made it through the majority of those tasks and was in the middle of blitzing peanuts and almonds for the torta Barozzi when Ainsley pushed through the swinging door separating the kitchen from the dining room.

Ainsley strode across the space, quickly closing the gap between them, and stood with hands on hips until the noise of the blender stopped. "Gabriella, we need to talk."

Gabi glanced briefly at the intruder but kept her focus on her task. "If you're going to be back here, you'll need to tie up your hair. The rules apply to everyone." She'd already wasted enough time that morning talking to her father about the arrangement with Gustare Foods, rehashing it with Ainsley wasn't going to get the kitchen lunch-ready, and it certainly wasn't going to make the situation better.

Ainsley slipped an elastic off her wrist and pulled back her hair, but that didn't deter her from completing her mission. "Can we step into the office please?"

Absolutely fucking ridiculous. Gabi didn't have time for girl talk about their feelings in the middle of morning prep, but apparently the Queen of the Dining Room wasn't going to give up until she'd said her piece. She threw her hands up in defeat. The torta Barozzi would have to wait. "Okay, fine."

She led Ainsley into the little office space and closed the door behind them. No need for the guys in the kitchen to hear their conversation. "Are you going to tell me what the hell you're stomping into my kitchen about?"

"You can't pull that kind of crap in front of the staff." The fire in Ainsley's eyes gave them a sexy glow. Under any other circumstances, Gabi would find her downright hot.

"What kind of crap?"

Ainsley narrowed her eyes. "Do you think I'm an idiot?"

There was no way Gabi was going to show her cards on that one. "Do you always answer a question with a question?"

"I'm not joking here, Gabriella. We have to present a united front to the staff."

"Danielle has been my friend since we were kids. We grew up on the same street." Gabi shook her head. "I'm not going to stop talking to her because you say so."

"She's an employee of D'Angelo's, and therefore staff. We must look like a team if we want this to work."

"If we want what to work? You pushing me out of my family's business?" Rage pounded in Gabi's ears. Now who was acting like the other was an idiot?

Ainsley's eyes narrowed. "Listen, I didn't know who you were when we hooked up the other night. I know we have to pivot due to our professional situation, but I really had a good time with you that night. I thought you were funny and sweet. Turns out you're just a jerk." She shook her head and her expression hardened. Stubbornly standing her ground. "Anyway, despite what you may think about me, I'm here to help you."

"Help me?" Gabi spat out the words. "I was on track to take over D'Angelo's after my father retired, and you've helped yourself to half of that gig, so you'll excuse me if I'm not ready to be besties. You inserted yourself into the situation and it's great that you say you want to help me, but I'm not interested in helping you. And we need more than a pivot. Just forget our hookup ever happened." She opened the office door and indicated it was time for Ainsley to exit. She was done with the conversation.

"Fine by me," Ainsley said over her shoulder on her way out. "I need to get myself organized out front anyway. Lots of work to do out there to get things up to Gustare Foods' standards."

"Right." Gabi could feel the pulse in her neck. She needed to get this woman out of her kitchen. "I get it. You're superior, we suck. Yadda, yadda, yadda."

Ainsley stopped short of pushing through the swinging doors and spun to face Gabi. "You know, when I saw you at the party and put two and two together, I really thought we could be friends even though we'd...you know." She shook her head as if to dismiss any remaining thoughts about the night they spent together. "I know if we worked together, we could totally do something great here."

"My family has been doing something great here for decades, but thanks anyway," Gabi snapped. "You do what you need to do out there, and I'll handle things back here. We'll coexist and everything will be just fine."

For the briefest moment, Ainsley looked like she was going to say more, but to Gabi's relief she finally disappeared through the swinging doors. *She'd thought they could be friends.* Business Management Barbie was too much. Gabi shook her head to clear it of all that nonsense. She had actual restaurant work to do.

CHAPTER FOUR

Ainsley flipped through the papers on her clipboard, but the lists that normally brought her a sense of calm and order were just not doing the trick. The words were swimming around on the page while her mind wandered off to rehash the morning's events. It wasn't that she expected Gabriella to welcome her with open arms, but she at least thought they would keep up some semblance of professionalism. Apparently, Gabriella hadn't got the memo that manners were always in style.

What had become of the funny, sexy woman Ainsley had met at the bar? Suddenly it was like they had never shared that delicious night at all. There was one minute of Miss Onion Tits where things between them teetered on the edge of *odd coincidence*, and then it all fell apart. Her core fluttered at the image of Gabriella standing there in her bra, gorgeous eyes full of concern about her blouse. Now it seemed that woman was just gone. Well, not the sexy part. She still had that going for her. Especially the way her eyes lit up when she was defending her kitchen. Passionate. But no. That wasn't important here.

Ainsley had a job to do, and she took her work very seriously. That didn't mean Gabriella had any right to call her names. She certainly didn't deserve *Corporate Stooge Boss Lady*. That was harsh.

Gabriella hadn't been at the restaurant the day Ainsley had met with Mr. D'Angelo to get the lay of the land. It was Mr. D'Angelo who had shown her around and reviewed their operating procedures with her—if you could call them "procedures." For the most part, the restaurant seemed to embrace a "just get it done" method of operating. Nothing formal was written down, or even in place as far as Ainsley could gather. The people were great. The vibe was positive. But if the restaurant was going to meet Gustare Foods' standards, some major changes would have to occur. Ainsley definitely had her work cut out. Especially when it came to comanaging with Gabriella for the next few months.

Everyone else with whom she'd interacted had been friendly and treated her with respect. Mr. D'Angelo and his brother, Sal, Danielle the daytime bartender, even the servers at the meeting that morning. What the hell was the deal with Gabriella?

The lunch rush had given Ainsley the perfect chance to see firsthand how the servers' routines worked, or maybe didn't work in the case of their habit of doling out straws and coffee creamer cups by the handfuls. That was a definite Gustare Foods no-no, and she would have to address that at the next server meeting. She managed to make a note about it in the margin of her Dining Room Procedures checklist before her mind wandered back to what was going on in the kitchen.

Was Gabriella going to be popping back into the dining room regularly to undermine her? The possibility had Ainsley's stomach jumping with nerves. The prospect of having to deal with her attitude was daunting. But also a little exciting. Because between the bossiness and the entitlement and those deep-brown eyes you could get lost in, the whole situation was somewhat confusing.

A crowd coming through the door pulled Ainsley's focus back to reality. At almost two o'clock, lunch should be drawing to a close, and there were no parties on the schedule, yet nine retirees were currently pushing two tables together in the corner of the dining room nearest the server station.

Ainsley grabbed Danielle who was bussing some of the tables where customers had recently left. "Do you want me to ask Jane if she can stick around a while to help with this party?"

"What party? Is something coming in?" Danielle paused midtask and wiped her hands on the bar towel hanging from her belt loop.

"Something already has." Ainsley tipped her head in the direction of the group settling in their seats. "I'm talking about the elderly group over there."

Danielle flicked her gaze over to the animated group at the combined table before going back to wiping down the one in front of her. "Oh, don't worry about that. I'll have help."

As if on cue, Gabriella came out of the kitchen carrying a tray with two large plates of antipasto and delivered them to the table just as Jane arrived with drinks for everyone.

"What the…" Ainsley marched across the dining room and waited—arms crossed and foot tapping—for Gabriella to greet everyone by name and crack a few jokes before leaving them again. "What is happening here?" Ainsley fell into step with her, but Gabriella stopped short of the kitchen doors. It was clear she didn't want Ainsley following her in.

"Customer service?"

"I'm serious. There aren't any parties on the schedule." Ainsley held out her tablet as evidence. "Yet you obviously knew they were coming in. All parties with a reservation need to be listed on the schedule."

"Let me see." Gabriella's brow furrowed as she took the tablet and poked at the screen. "Uh-huh. There you go."

"Great job, Einstein." Ainsley hoped her tone held every last drop of sarcasm she intended. "You added a party of ten on the schedule at this time every Monday for…" She scrolled through the calendar. "The rest of the year."

"That's because this group comes in every Monday, plays cards all afternoon, then has dinner together."

"Every Monday?"

"That's what it says on the schedule." Gabriella flashed a snarky half-smile that made something in Ainsley's core stir.

Bitchiness usually did not have that kind of impact, but... *No.* There were procedures in place for a reason, and Gabriella was going to have to face that. Ainsley smirked right back. "And you know we'll have to charge them the fifteen percent service charge for parties of more than eight guests."

The mirth dropped from Gabriella's face as if she'd been slapped. "Absolutely not. These people are some of our most loyal regulars. They've been eating here since the place opened, and they're senior citizens. I'm not charging them some ridiculous, made-up fee for nothing. Fuck Gustare Foods. This is my restaurant. Don't you dare add an extra cent to their bill." She didn't give Ainsley a chance to react, just spun on her heel and shoved through the doors into the kitchen.

Ainsley briefly considered chasing after her, but activity in the server station caught her attention instead.

"Sir. Sir, you can't do that," she said, rushing over to the station where the old man was helping himself to a refill of his Diet Coke from the fountain. "You can't be back here. This area is for employees only. Please go back to your table and I'll happily bring you a pitcher."

The man shook his head and let out a low, rumbling laugh while he continued to fill his glass. "Young lady, we already have pitchers at our table. Jane brought them by before she left. But I like my soda fresh out of the fountain, and it's no problem. I don't mind fetching it myself."

The last thing Ainsley—or D'Angelo's for that matter—needed was an old guy slipping on an ice cube in the server station and breaking his hip all because he needed fresh-from-the-fountain soda. "You're our guest. Please just let us take care of you, sir."

He waved a wrinkled and weathered hand at her. "So formal. It's Vic. And that beauty over there in the pink blouse is my beautiful bride, Ida. I've been bringing her here since we started dating. Before Bruno D'Angelo took over from his father in the nineties. Been friends with Bruno since then too."

The man was rambling on while Ainsley escorted him back to the table, but she didn't mind. She was just relieved to have avoided a liability claim. "Well, Vic, it's very nice to meet you. I'm Ainsley. I'll tell you what I'm going to do. I'm going to hang out right there in the server station all afternoon and if you need another refill and Danielle's not around, you just give me a wave and I'll hop right over to help you out. No need for you to get up, and certainly no reason for you to have to go back into the server station again. I will take care of you."

"That's just wonderful. Thank you." Vic gave her a toothy grin before announcing to the table, "Everyone, meet Ainsley, the new girl."

The table erupted with various greetings. Ida said, "Isn't she a pretty girl," and everyone agreed. Ainsley's cheeks flushed warmly.

"I knew her first!"

Ainsley looked up to see Ruby joining the group, a proud smile gracing her face. "Ruby? What are you doing here?"

Ruby looped her purse over the back of her chair and plopped down in her seat. "I'm here to play cards. These are my friends and I'm here to kick their butts."

"Good luck with that," the man to Vic's left muttered.

"But why didn't you tell me that you would be here?" Her landlord just strolling into her place of work to join the seniors' card club that had taken over her dining room totally tracked with the day Ainsley was having.

"I didn't want to make you nervous on your first day, dear," Ruby replied simply before addressing the others at the table. "Are we going to deal the cards or flap our gums all day?"

* * *

Waiting for Vic to signal for a refill, Ainsley made the most of her afternoon in the server station, reviewing the setup of the dining room space and comparing the server procedures already in place to the Gustare Foods' server checklist. She'd compiled copious notes on the improvements she'd need to make.

To her relief, Gabriella had stayed in the kitchen, but that reprieve suddenly came to a halt at dinner time. Gabriella trailed behind Danielle, carrying a second tray of meals for the card club. Ainsley glanced at the clock—four o'clock on the nose. Still a little breathing room before the dinner rush kicked up. It didn't matter. Gabriella could help Danielle serve the group without Ainsley paying them any attention. Instead, she would focus on the servers coming on shift, making sure she introduced herself to everyone and observing their work in the dining room.

Not a minute too soon. The very first thing she witnessed was the young server, who'd introduced herself as Kelsey, scoop a cupful of ice right out of the bin using the same glass she then filled with soda to deliver to a customer.

"Oh, Kelsey, don't use the glass to scoop ice. Let's use the actual scoop instead." Ainsley pointed helpfully in the direction of the tool dangling from a hook on the side of the ice bin. "I know it seems nitpicky, but it's a health-code violation. If the glass breaks, we'd have shards mixed in with the ice. It would be a terrible mess."

"Yeah, okay," Kelsey answered flatly and cracked her gum. Gum chewing on shift would be the next violation they would cover. "But these glasses are plastic. They're not even actual glass."

"Have you never seen hard plastic shatter? Still ends in shards." Ainsley made a note on her clipboard to remember to discuss positive attitudes at the next server meeting. "Use the scoop."

"Whatever." Kelsey shrugged and filled another glass, this time using the approved utensil, but when she was finished, she left it in the bin instead of returning it to the hook.

"You can't just leave the scoop sitting in the ice. That's a health-code violation too," Ainsley called after her, but Kelsey didn't even slow down much less look back. She blew out an exasperated sigh and hung the scoop back in its proper place.

"A little hitch in the revolution?" Gabriella leaned against the entrance to the server station, a smart-ass grin on her smug face. Of course she would catch that failed exchange. How many hits was Ainsley going to take on her first day?

"I'll add it to my list for the server meeting, don't worry." Ainsley kept her eyes trained on her clipboard. She didn't dare meet Gabriella's gaze for fear she'd see the disappointment she was feeling written across her face.

"I told you we do pretty fine around here as is. We don't need Gustare Foods coming in here and changing things up. We're good, but thanks anyway."

"You're…good?" Ainsley felt the tendons in her neck strain and twitch. Of all the pompous, mother-freaking…who did this woman think she was, and why the hell did she believe her restaurant was immune to state regulations? Gabriella was living in some kind of dream world if she thought their operations didn't need cleaning up. "You think everything's fine, and you have no need for me? I'm just, what? Spewing total nonsense? You think I don't know what I'm talking about?"

"I don't know about spewing total nonsense," Gabriella said, punctuated by a dramatic eye roll. "But, yeah, I do think everything's fine here."

Ainsley's gaze moved from the ice scoop still swinging on its hook, to the soda machine that was obviously in need of a good cleaning. It was clear D'Angelo's was Gabriella's world, that her family and their business were the most important things in her life, but when it came to the reality of the situation she was seeing things through rose-colored glasses. The restaurant just needed a bit of a revamp—a little polish and shine—and it could be everything Gabriella believed it was. The truth was, that level of quality just wasn't there at the moment, and it was Ainsley's job to get it back. She wasn't about to let some entitled, bratty grump stand in her way.

"You're completely fooling yourself, Gabriella. Things at D'Angelo's are not fine." She swept an open arm in the direction of the soda machine. "See those crusty patches of brown crud on the nozzles? That's a sign that the machine hasn't been properly cleaned in at least two weeks. And that's a health-code violation."

Gabriella frowned. "It's one machine with a little soda on it. Our restaurant is clean overall. No rodents or vermin or anything disgusting like that."

"A restaurant doesn't have to be disgusting to violate health code. Food health and safety regulations are in place to keep things from getting to that point."

"So the server station needs a good cleaning. It's not going to set off a total downward spiral for the entirety of D'Angelo's." Gabriella shrugged. "We can do that by close tonight. No big deal."

"No big deal? That's honestly what you think? Come here." Ainsley stiffened her jaw to ward off the throbbing in her temples as she linked elbows with Gabriella. "Come with me."

She marched her through the dining room and into the kitchen. A quick survey of the place gave her ample opportunities for a starting point, but she selected the food-prep area.

"See this spray bottle here on the table?" Ainsley let go of Gabriella, to gesture at the offensive item. "It's a problem."

"You were just on my case about how we need to clean." Gabriella scowled. "So why is a spray bottle of cleaning solution a problem?"

"How do you know it's cleaning solution?"

Gabriella squinted at her like she'd grown a second head. "Because it's in one of the spray bottles we use for cleaning."

"And how does everyone else know it's cleaning solution?" Ainsley asked, a generous prompt to lead Gabriella to the correct answer.

"Because it's in one of the spray bottles we use for cleaning," Gabriella repeated in a much more annoyed tone than the first time she said it. She was still missing the point.

"But someone might not know that because it's *not labeled*, and that's a violation. All spray bottles need to be labeled, and besides that, it really shouldn't be left sitting here on a food-prep surface."

"Well, I know that. Of course I know that. Someone probably just set it there for a second and will be right back for it." Gabriella snatched the bottle off the table. "Okay. Labels. Got it."

"Oh, that's not all," Ainsley said, leading her to the walk-in cooler. She wasn't one hundred percent sure of what she would find, but she had a hunch there would be something she could call out. One step inside and...bingo. "You can't store anything on the floor in here. It's a violation. You need to get that box of peppers on a shelf."

"They usually are." Gabriella sounded defensive as she quickly moved to get the box onto one of the stainless-steel shelving units. She looked a little unnerved. "I don't know how that happened."

"And this container here." Ainsley poked a finger at a Rubbermaid food-storage container filled with kidney beans. "Violation."

"What are you talking about? It has a secure lid, it's *on a shelf*. It's even clearly labeled 'kidney beans.' There's nothing wrong with that."

"Food must be stored in commercial-grade containers, not regular household ones. And that label should have a date on it. Violation." Point made, Ainsley spun on her heel and exited the walk-in.

Behind her Gabriella groaned, but she followed along.

As they continued through the kitchen, Ainsley pointed out other infractions. "Cooks wearing bracelets and rings—violation. Employee beverages sitting with no lid on a food-prep surface—violation. No hand-washing instructions posted by that sink—violation."

"Oh my God. We all know how to wash our hands."

"Of course you do." Ainsley balled her fists on her hips. She was not about to back down now. "But the health code states the sign has to be posted, and if an inspector comes in here and it's not, you're going to get dinged."

"I think you're making a mountain out of a molehill." Gabriella shook her head. "These are all tiny little things you're pointing out."

"But a bunch of little things during an inspection add up and can cause big trouble."

"This is ridiculous. We've never had a problem with health inspections in the past."

Ainsley shrugged, knowing all too well how easily the little things could trip you up during a food and safety visit. "Health inspectors don't usually show up unannounced unless they get a complaint. But if they do, violations like the ones I just pointed out can lead to fines or even an order to shut the place down until the problems are corrected."

"Shut down?" Gabriella's jaw dropped. "For this shit? You have got to be kidding."

"I am not." Finally, Ainsley seemed to be getting through to her. "And once word gets out that your restaurant has been shut down for health-code violations, your reputation is likely to take a hit, so you can expect a dip in sales once you are finally able to reopen. Do you still think it's no big deal?"

For the first time since they'd met, Gabriella's expression was completely devoid of its usual bravado. Brow furrowed, she chewed on her bottom lip before finally tipping her head in the direction of her office. A silent invitation for Ainsley to join her in the more private space.

"Okay." Gabriella closed the door behind them. Now that it was just the two of them, she looked even more deflated than before. "I get it. We need to straighten up and fly right. You win. What do you want me to do?"

At last, a bit of rationality in the situation. It was about time.

"I want you to give me a chance to make some changes," Ainsley said, crossing her arms. "I want you to stop calling me names and acting like I don't know what I'm talking about. I want you to stop making my job harder than it has to be."

Gabriella scrubbed her hands over her face as if agreeing to these simple things was stressful to her. "Fine," she mumbled.

"Fine?" That was all the response this woman was going to give her?

"Well, I can't make any promises about the name-calling, but I'll try." Gabriella shrugged, but there was a twinkle of teasing in her eye. It was a glimmer of the woman Ainsley had met that first night, and a huge improvement over the *ready to pull her hair out* look she had been wearing a moment before, but then she quickly sobered again. "Look, we're obviously going to have to figure out a way to work together, so let's stick to you handling things out front and me holding it down back here. That way we can avoid tripping over each other while we take care of business."

It wasn't exactly the result Ainsley had hoped for, but it was a start and much better than constantly butting heads. It was only her first day on the job and this would have to do. For now. There was plenty of time to turn things around. But still, there was one point she wanted to make.

"And?" She raised her eyebrows at Gabriella, hopeful that she would take the bait.

Gabriella blew out what seemed to be a sigh of surrender. "And I'll correct the things you just pointed out back here."

"Excellent," Ainsley said as she opened the door to exit the office. "If you need me, I'll be out front.

Sometimes you had to take the small victories.

CHAPTER FIVE

Gabi greeted Wednesday morning with a groan, compliments of the pinch in her lower back. She wasn't surprised by the aches and pains. After Ainsley had basically put the fear of God in her, Gabi had worked doubly hard to make sure everything was in order and gave the whole place a deep clean. It was nearly midnight by the time she'd finally left the restaurant on Monday night. Even though the restaurant was closed on Tuesdays, she still needed to be there to unload the morning delivery. Normally she went home after the inventory was taken and various other administrative tasks were complete, but this week she'd stayed longer to finish up the work she'd begun the night before.

Which was why, when she managed to roll out of bed, she went directly to click on the coffee maker and prayed the carton of milk hadn't expired. It was absurd really—she loved good food and loved to cook, but besides the pint of half-and-half, there were eggs, butter, American cheese, and a handful of condiments in her fridge. She ate most meals at the restaurant or at her nonna's. It was time to pick up some groceries.

The first swallow of scalding joe brought Gabi's senses to life. A glance at her phone showed she had less than forty-five minutes until she needed to be back at D'Angelo's starting her morning routine. And starting another day with her front-of-house counterpart, Ainsley Becker.

The kitchen might well be in better shape, but Gabi's pride still stung as she thought about all the code violations Ainsley had spotted. Pop had always been a stickler for doing things by the book and keeping everything up to code. He would've been pissed if he'd been there and witnessed Gabi's lazy mistakes. He would probably say that was an example of exactly they needed Gustare Foods' help. She wouldn't slip up again.

It wasn't just the violations still gnawing away at Gabi, it was the fact that Boss Lady Barbie probably felt a new confidence about their working relationship. Like she had a leg up on the situation now just because she'd rattled off a few rules. And now Gabi would have to contend with that too.

Although, there was that moment right before Ainsley started pointing out offenses, when her eyes lit up with a fire and a fury and drew herself up to a serious *woman in charge* posture. A look that Gabi couldn't deny was damn sexy and drew her thoughts right back to their night together. A night that Gabi was doing her damnedest to forget. Talk about confusing—one minute Gabi had wanted to slap that damn know-it-all look right off her face, the next she'd felt the urge to get it on with her right there in the server station.

She drained the last of the coffee and rinsed her mug out in the sink before heading back to her bedroom to dress. It was time to get those thoughts out of her head and face the day.

Face the day with her new, and sometimes sexy, coworker. *Dammit.*

* * *

Gabi's morning routine in D'Angelo's kitchen was a salve to her frayed nerves. The one time she'd ventured out to the server station to grab a Diet Coke she noticed a deep cleaning had apparently taken place out there as well. Must have occurred first thing that morning since the *crusty brown crud*—as Ainsley had so eloquently named it—that had still been present on the machine when she'd left on Monday was gone.

There were some other changes too. A helpful sign with an arrow pointing to the scoop had been taped to the lid of the ice bin. And a small whiteboard had been fashioned into a chart labeled "side work" with additional responsibilities assigned to each of the servers who would be on shift over the course of the day.

At least Ainsley seemed to be holding up her end of their deal and keeping things up to code in the front of the house. Maybe they'd be able to find a way to have a decent working relationship after all. Except for the fact that Ainsley was a part of Gustare Foods. Gabi still couldn't shake the feeling that there was something weird about their interest in her family's restaurant. As she sliced tomatoes, cucumbers, and onions for the side salads, she turned it over in her mind again, but it still didn't make things any clearer.

She trayed up the salads, labeled them with the date, and got them onto the rack in the walk-in, then she wandered over to the service window to see what Ainsley was up to in the dining room. Probably just bossing the waitstaff around and being superior about everything.

Even though it was only a little after ten a.m., Jane was occupying one of the sunny tables by the windows at the front of the restaurant, wrapping silverware while she waited for the lunch shift to start. The usual. Just the way Gabi liked it. Jane would never put up with Ainsley's Gustare Foods crap. She knew the value of a mom-and-pop shop and what being a good neighbor meant. Jane had been with them for as long as Gabi could remember. Her daughter had even worked at D'Angelo's for a while before she married and moved away. Yeah. Jane was definitely one person Gabi could count on to stand up to Gustare Foods' mumbo jumbo.

Ah, here we go. Ainsley sat down at the table across from Jane and said something that made the server smile. Gabi couldn't hear their words, but their body language appeared open and friendly. Jane responded but kept at her task. She shook her head, but her expression appeared thoughtful before she continued speaking with Ainsley. The conversation seemed to conclude on a positive note as Ainsley stood again, the women shook hands, and traded agreeable smiles before Ainsley walked away.

It wasn't until Jane finished with the silverware and carried the bin to the server station that Gabi hustled into the dining room under the guise of refilling her Diet Coke hoping to catch her alone.

"What was that all about?" Gabi asked casually as she followed the instructions on the sign and used the scoop to fill her cup. *Take that, Ainsley.*

"What's that, dear?" Jane asked as she bustled around the station checking supplies for lunch.

"Your tête-à-tête with our new dining room manager. Did she ask you to swear allegiance to Gustare Foods or something like that?"

"Gabi." Jane shot her a wary look. "*Who Moved My Cheese?*"

"Who moved your...what?" Gabi tried to make the question make sense in her head. "No one. All cheese is in the walk-in where we always keep it. Properly labeled and dated, of course." Was this some kind of Gustare Foods test?

"It's a book, dear. About change in the workplace." Jane continued to survey the sugar packets, mayo, and mustard packets. "*Who Moved My Cheese?* It was written quite a few years back, but it still rings true. I think you should read it. Sometimes change is a good and necessary thing."

Gabi's stomach twisted. Ainsley had gotten to Jane. "Dang it. Did she pull some kind of Gustare Foods mind-meld thing on you? Is that what the two of you were doing over there?"

Jane blew out a sigh that indicated she was out of patience with the conversation. "If you really must know, she sat down with me and said she respected my opinion as the senior server here and wanted to know what I thought about Gustare Foods' policy of banning straws from the restaurant. I told her I didn't think it would fly with our customers." Jane shrugged. "She said she'd think a little more on it and try to find a compromise."

"A compromise?" That didn't sound like the Ainsley Gabi knew. Then again, she didn't really know Ainsley.

"Yes. And then she asked me to take a look at the side-work chart and let her know if I thought it needed any adjustments. So, I said I would. That was it." Jane gave her a pointed look. "No brainwashing. Now if it's okay with you, I need to finish stocking the station before the hungry people come in for lunch."

As Jane headed on to her next task, Gabi replayed her words. She definitely said Ainsley was going to try to find a compromise to make Gustare Foods' suggestions work. Good thing too. The regulars would never stand for D'Angelo's going straw-free, not to mention the Monday card club would probably stage a riot. But Gabi hadn't missed the way Ainsley had complimented Jane to get on her good side. Very clever. Maybe she should have let Ainsley take their straws. Then let her suffer the consequences of her actions with their customers. It did sound like a front-of-house problem, after all.

So what if Ainsley had won over Jane? It was just one person. And front of the house. That went along with their agreement—Ainsley handled the dining room. Gabi handled the kitchen. It was fine. The staff still knew Gabi was really the one in charge at D'Angelo's. *Her family's restaurant.*

She couldn't let herself get swept up in worrying about this right now. She had to get back into the kitchen and get ready for lunch. She needed to...chop something. Maybe that would help.

* * *

It was less than an hour later when Ainsley sauntered into the kitchen, despite her promise to keep her business to the front of house. She seemed especially interested in Gabi's work, peering across the steel prep table, her eyebrow quirked up in judgment.

"These are the meatballs you have on the menu at three for five dollars?" Ainsley frowned as she leaned across the stainless-steel table, resting her elbows on it and settling in as if she was expecting a conversation. "They're so small."

Gabi sucked in a deep breath. She was not going to let Ainsley poke a hole in her composure this early in the day. She could play nice. "No, these are not those meatballs from the menu. These are the meatballs for the wedding soup. And get your body off my workspace. Very unhygienic. Probably some kind of a health-code violation too."

"Oh, sorry." She stood up. Her face clouded with disappointment, and she took a few steps back as if to make up for her transgressions. "I wasn't thinking."

Was she going to be all sad-and-hurt feelings now? What a piece of work. Gabi sighed. "It's okay. It's just that there are rules in my kitchen, and those rules are in place for a reason."

She noticed Ainsley's eyebrow quirk up when she'd said, "My kitchen." As if she was doubting her. Or laughing at her. *What the fuck?* It *was* her kitchen. Back here she was the boss, no matter what Ainsley Becker and Gustare Foods thought. "Whatever. What are you doing back here anyway?"

Ainsley stood up a little straighter. "I was hoping to learn some of the back-of-house procedures. There's nothing for me to do out front at this time of the day anyway."

"You back here to spy on me or something?"

"I just told you, I'm here to learn." Ainsley frowned, but she spread her hands open in front of her in a *nothing to hide* gesture. "Not spy. You know what? Forget it."

As Ainsley turned to leave the kitchen, Gabi fully intended to shift her focus back to the task at hand, but instead of thinking about rolling perfectly sized mini-meatballs, her mind filled with thoughts of the promise she'd made to her father. How she agreed she'd do things his way and give Gustare Foods a chance. As Ainsley had shown signs of compromise in the dining room that morning, maybe Gabi could be a little more open to giving her the benefit of the doubt.

"You ever make wedding soup?" she asked just before Ainsley pushed through the swinging door to the dining room. "You know anything about it?"

Ainsley paused as if considering a choice, but then turned back to Gabi's workstation. "I know it's delicious."

"Wait until you've had *our* wedding soup." Gabi pinched a practiced measure of the meat mixture between her fingers and started rolling again. "I'll show you delicious. Grab an apron and wash your hands."

When Ainsley rejoined her, Gabi showed her how to use a teaspoon to measure the mix and get the size of the meatballs correct.

"How come I have to use the measuring spoon, but you're freehanding it?"

"I've been doing this since I was eighteen." Gabi shrugged. "I can eyeball a mini-meatball with the best of them."

"Color me impressed." And to Gabi's surprise, Ainsley actually looked like she meant it. "You make them so consistently the same size. That's seriously a skill."

It was an actual compliment from Ainsley Becker and it caused a warmth to creep up Gabi's neck behind her ears. "Thank you," Gabi replied, but she kept her eyes on the meat. It was weird the way that feeling had sneaked up on her—an urge to let her guard down. A change of subject was called for. "Do you know why it's called wedding soup?"

"Because it's served at weddings?" Ainsley rolled a carefully measured portion between her hands.

"This could become a real chicken or egg discussion, I guess," Gabi said with a chuckle. "*Minestra maritata* is the actual name which doesn't mean 'wedding soup,' but rather 'married soup' because of the marriage of the ingredients—the meat and the leafy greens."

"Minestra maritata," Ainsley repeated, her full lips shaping each syllable with concentration.

"When I first learned that—when I was little—I used to think about the foods as a bride and groom. Like a meatball wearing a tuxedo and top hat, and a spinach leaf clad in all white with a lacy veil," Gabi confessed. "I pictured a big silver soup spoon standing in front of them officiating."

Ainsley laughed—a light twittering sound just a blush away from a giggle. "That's so cute. I can see it now—they could honeymoon in a big pot of broth. It could get steamy."

"I see what you did there." Gabi laughed along with her. She had almost forgotten that Ainsley had a sense of humor. At least there was that much to indicate she wasn't *completely* terrible, even if she had butted in on managing the front of the restaurant.

Right.

They weren't friends. They were just two people who worked at the same place, and even that was just for the short-term. Only until things around D'Angelo's settled down and Gustare Foods and Ainsley Becker went on their merry way. She needed to get this instructional session on soup back on track. She placed two large cast-iron skillets on the stovetop. "The soup isn't going to cook itself. We'd better get back to it."

Confusion registered on Ainsley's face, but she continued producing mini-meatballs anyway. "What are those for?"

"We're going to sear the meatballs before they go into the broth," Gabi explained. She could still remember the day her father had taught her the secret to Nonna's minestra maritata: searing the meatballs. She held many moments like that one in her heart. Her and her pop in D'Angelo's kitchen as he handed down family recipes. The best times. "Browning them adds flavor."

"OOO?"

"Yeah, it's pretty delicious."

"No, what is it?"

"What is what?"

"The OOO." Ainsley frowned, which was not the reaction Gabi was used to when she was cooking for someone. "The Order of Operations."

"No one says that."

"They do at Gustare Foods."

"Please tell me you're not serious right now."

"What? It's part of my job to learn procedures and review them for efficiency." Ainsley pulled a small notebook from her pocket and flipped it open, pen at the ready.

"Why does Gustare Foods want to take the joy out of cooking? This isn't a procedure, it's a family recipe. This is love." She flicked her gaze at the notebook. "Besides, I'm not wild about you writing down Nonna's recipe."

"It's literally what they sent me here to do." She looked so earnest.

"I couldn't possibly give it up. I barely even know you." Gabi was teasing now. She couldn't resist.

Ainsley opened her mouth as if she was going to protest further, but then she shut it again and simply tucked the notebook and pen away. Those sexy lips curled into a playful smile, and she held up her empty hands as if in surrender. "Fair enough. We'll do this one off the record. Please, teach me the secret of your nonna's minestra maritata."

Gabi liked that she used the Italian name for the soup, and that she was willing to play along and buck her Gustare Foods duties. Maybe there was some good in that front-store stealer after all.

CHAPTER SIX

The lunch rush was slowing to more of a trickle, with just a few tables finishing their meals, and Ainsley was finally taking a minute to breathe. She sat at the bar with a tall glass of iced tea and stared at her post-lunch checklists, but her mind kept traveling back to her time that morning in the kitchen with Gabriella.

She'd had fun making wedding soup—minestra maritata—as Gabriella had taught her. They had both had fun. Together. Laughing as they rolled meatballs, combined ingredients, and ultimately produced a delicious pot of soup, if she did say so herself. Was it possible that she and Gabriella were becoming... friends?

Sure, they'd had a rocky few days, but if she looked at that first night they'd shared, there was definitely some potential. That night—the way Gabriella looked in only her lacy bra and boy-short panties, the chemistry sizzling between them as they tumbled between the sheets exploring each other's bodies and riding their pleasure right over the edge again and again. The memories had been playing nonstop on a loop ever since. When they met again the following night, Ainsley had thought maybe that was a chance for the connection between them to grow. But instead, Gabriella had insisted they put the past behind them and just forget it ever happened. She'd shut it down with Ainsley having no say in the matter. And from there things had become downright frosty between them.

The morning making soup had given Ainsley hope that maybe they had crossed a threshold. The sunshine had burst through the dark gray clouds. Finally, it seemed Gabi had dropped that gruff defense that had been her mood since Ainsley had arrived at D'Angelo's.

She still wasn't sure why Gabriella insisted on making her job so hard. Everything she'd done at the restaurant thus far was Gustare Foods' protocol. While she had to admit D'Angelo's seemed to function just fine, even without Gustare Foods' help, she was there to do a job, and that was what she was going to do. The way Gabriella had butted heads with her at every turn made it pretty clear that she wasn't thrilled about getting on board with their program. And her stubbornness regarding being in charge and calling all the shots indicated she was far from ready to give up her position. It was almost as if she didn't know that Gustare Foods was going to—

"Let's just pull a few tables together over here," Gabriella called out from across the dining room to the group entering the restaurant. Suddenly, a dozen people were moving tables and chairs and making themselves at home with Gabriella smiling and settling in with them.

Are you kidding me? Ainsley poked at her tablet. Nope. No parties scheduled for that afternoon, but obviously Gabriella had expected this gathering. Had they not literally just had this fight?

Never mind. She wasn't going to ruin their goodwill just because Gabriella and her friends were yucking it up in the middle of the dining room. She would just go back to her checklists and mind her own business. Or her own *portion* of the business, which was the dining room in case Gabriella had forgotten.

"Hey, Ainsley, could you fill a couple of beer pitchers and bring them over?"

Ainsley spun on her barstool slowly to fix Gabriella with a death glare, but Gabriella wasn't paying her any attention. She seemed to be completely enthralled with whatever the twenty-something redhead seated to her right was saying. And possibly what she was wearing. It was early April in Pittsburgh, Pennsylvania. Seriously, it couldn't be more than sixty degrees outside, and this young woman was dressed in a denim miniskirt and a flimsy camisole that laced up the front, showing way more cleavage than was necessary. It was practically just a bra. Ridiculous. And the way the Little Red was gazing back at Gabriella was like she hung the moon. All long-lash-batting heart emoji eyes. Gabriella's ego was probably growing by leaps and bounds, which was the last thing she needed. Or at least it was the last thing Ainsley needed.

It wasn't that Ainsley was jealous about the way they were interacting. Gabriella was a single woman and could be flirty with whomever she wanted. They'd had a one-night stand— one that Gabriella insisted they completely forget. They had no claim on the other. They were not even friends. Gabriella flirting with someone else was totally fine.

"Are you going to take these, or do you want me to do it?" Danielle interrupted her thoughts as she pushed two plastic pitchers of draft beer across the bar. "Looks like Jane already dropped off glasses."

As if she was supposed to just drop everything and serve drinks to Gabriella and her friends. To Gabriella and Little Red, now throwing her head back and laughing at something Gabriella had said, as if it was the funniest thing she'd ever heard in her short life. *Oh my God*, was her hand on Gabriella's thigh? Ainsley was supposed to just go over there and set a pitcher of beer between them while they flirted?

She could go over there between them with a pitcher of beer.

She grabbed the pitchers and, with a smile plastered on her face, carried them over to the table like she was the St. Pauli Girl on the beer label, a buxom wench carrying huge froth-filled steins. She wedged herself between the two and set the beer down before turning to Gabriella.

"I didn't see a party on the schedule for this afternoon. Did you forget what we talked about? Could you not have at least mentioned in the hours we spent together this morning that you would be hosting a shindig in the dining room today?"

Gabriella's pleasant expression never wavered, but she hissed her response. "Can I speak to you over by the bar for a second?" When they were far enough away from the table to be out of earshot, Gabriella continued, "Is there some kind of problem?"

"Yes, there is, and I just very plainly told you what it was." Ainsley balled her fists on her hips. She wasn't about to back down. "We had an agreement—you were in charge of the kitchen, I'm in charge of the dining room. But here you are, blatantly disregarding one of the simplest rules. Reservations for parties larger than eight must be logged on the schedule. You clearly knew this group was coming. Hell, you seem to be the one in charge."

"Are you kidding me right now?" Gabriella shook her head and the wisps of dark-brown hair that had fallen from her bun danced around her face. "There are at least a dozen empty tables available should we happen to experience a two o'clock in the afternoon rush."

"You know that's not the point." Ainsley pinched the bridge of her nose. She could feel a headache coming on. "The point is how you continually disrespect me. How even when it seems like we're finally figuring out how to work together, you have to bring some hotsy-totsy in here and throw a party in the middle of the workday."

The corner of Gabriella's mouth hitched up in a smirk. "That's what this is about. I'll have you know Hailey is a member of the Slice of Italy Committee. That's all. Same as me. The *party* I'm hosting over there is a committee meeting, and we're doing some important work, so if it's okay with you, I'm going to get back to it."

She was acting like the words *Slice of Italy* should mean something, but Ainsley still felt like she was two steps behind. "What's the Slice of Italy Committee?"

"I'm sorry, all further questions will have to wait. I'm much too busy to entertain any more of them." Gabriella smirked. God, she was exasperating. "But I will tell you this—she really is just some girl on the committee."

She actually had the nerve to wink before she turned and went back to the meeting, leaving Ainsley with her unanswered questions and weird feelings that were definitely not jealousy-based—no matter what the head of the Slice of Italy Committee thought.

* * *

When Ainsley got home that evening, she knocked lightly on Ruby's door. A cheerful "Come on in," greeted her from the other side. She found Ruby knitting in the living room, humming along to the '80s station on the radio.

Ainsley plopped down on the sofa and blew out a long sigh.

"Oh my," Ruby exclaimed. "That was pitiful. Take a minute and listen to the song—she's saying girls just wanna have fun."

"I'm familiar with the song."

"You don't seem like a girl who wants to have fun." Ruby raised a curious eyebrow in her direction. "Although you look like a girl who *needs* to have fun."

Ainsley couldn't help the laugh that bubbled out of her. Leave it to Ruby to call a spade a spade. "It is a catchy song."

"It's a great song." Ruby slapped her thigh to emphasize her point. "One year at Slice of Italy they had a karaoke night and me and the gals from the bowling league did that one. Oh, what a hoot."

"The Slice of Italy Festival seems to be on everybody's mind today. You mentioned that before when I was admiring the pictures on your wall, so I was hoping you could tell me more about it. When is it?"

"The festival *was* held every June. But the last one was the summer of 2019, I'm afraid." Ruby pursed her lips and shook her head sadly. "Canceled for the pandemic in 2020 and never came back. But I hear they've got a group working to bring it back this year."

"What?" Ainsley didn't know why—she'd never attended Slice of Italy—but she was appalled. "Why did they stop having it?"

"Just lost its steam, I guess." Ruby's expression clouded with sadness. "The founder passed away that September after it was canceled. It was no small feat putting together a festival like that, and no one else stepped up to pick up the thread."

"That's so sad—for the founder and the neighborhood. It sounds like it was a heck of a festival. I mean, karaoke is always fun."

"Well, they didn't have karaoke every year, but there was always plenty of entertainment. Something different every night," Ruby said as she left her armchair and pulled a dusty photo album from the shelf. "Local bands, dance groups, and of course, the Miss Slice of Italy Pageant."

Ainsley digested that last bit of information while Ruby settled onto the couch beside her and opened the book. The colorful photos neatly arranged on the pages immediately drew her in. "That's a lot of people, and they all look like they're having the time of their lives."

"I'm telling you, year after year it drew a huge crowd." Ruby beamed.

"What's happening here?" She pointed at a picture of three people holding a slice of pizza in one hand and a prize ribbon in the other.

"The Best Slice in the 'Burgh Contest." Ruby clapped her hands "Restaurants from all around the Pittsburgh area would compete for the title. Most years D'Angelo's was one of the finalists. Same with Russo's. The food at the festival was heavenly. And, oh, the wine!"

"Sal D'Angelo's?"

"Of course. But not just his. All the local wineries would come. There were even a couple wineries from Ohio that made an appearance once or twice."

Ainsley flipped the page and ran her gaze across another set of photos: kids jumping in a castle-shaped bouncy house, a table of old women laughing and playing cards, a plate of cannoli dusted with powdered sugar that looked so delicious her stomach rumbled. Joy. Pages full of joy. "It looks like a really good time."

Ruby's face lit up with nostalgia. "It really was. Our neighborhood knows how to celebrate, believe you me. I hope they'll be able to get it up and running again. If they do, you should definitely check it out."

Ainsley thought about the last few places she'd lived. She didn't even know the names of her next-door neighbors at most of them. She could tell herself it was because she never really stuck around long enough to get to know anyone, but somehow that was a lie. It seemed like it had more to do with the Bloomfield's sense of community that she hadn't experienced anywhere else. Neighborhood pride—she could see it on the faces of the people in the photos and she could see it on Ruby too. Neighborhood pride was one of those old-timey concepts from the '60s or '70s that needed to make a comeback. It deserved a reboot. Ainsley had never experienced that feeling, so she'd never missed it. But now her heart ached a little and she was surprised to realize she wanted some of that for herself. "It sounds like something I wouldn't want to miss. I'll put it on my calendar."

What the heck? She'd still be in Bloomfield in June, so may as well partake in the local customs.

CHAPTER SEVEN

Dinner orders had been a nonstop deluge Saturday evening, which was great for business, but rough on the kitchen staff. Gabi had managed to keep her patience with the guys working the grill and the line, but barely, and by the time the rush ended and they finished cleaning the kitchen for the night, she was beat. She was still standing, but her good graces had called it a day.

Which is why when she strolled into the dining room to find that Ainsley hadn't finished the front-of-house close routine, she lost what little composure she had left. "What the hell have you been doing out here?" she growled. "Why aren't you done yet?"

Ainsley squinted at her with obvious disdain. "It was busy out here too tonight, you know. Where do you think the bulk of the dinner orders come from? We had almost two hundred people come through those doors tonight. I only just let the last of the servers leave after they finished up their side work." She sighed like she'd used the last of her own vim in response. "I get that you're tired, but I am too. All I have left to do is restocking the wine anyway."

Gabi was in no mood for it. Ainsley should be able to manage her time as well as her staff. No excuses. "If you wouldn't have spent forty-five minutes having that server sorority meeting, you would've had plenty of time to restock the wine, and we wouldn't be stuck here with one last thing to do at the end of the night after everyone else got to go home."

"Don't insult the servers like that. It's not like we were swapping gossip and painting each other's nails. I'm holding these training sessions to bring the staff up to speed on health-code serving standards, something they should know already since none of them are exactly new here except for one. And yet..."

"Oh, please. Our serving staff is fine. Even the new girl, Kelsey. We never get complaints, and the regulars love them all."

Ainsley slammed her clipboard down on the bar. "That's not the point." She blew out an exasperated breath. "Just give me your keys and go. I'll finish up then come back early to open in the morning."

"The last thing I want is to have to meet you here early in the morning. I already had to stay here late tonight. I'll just restock it myself." She spun on her heel and made a beeline for the cellar stairs, praying that Ainsley didn't follow.

It was a mean thing to say, she knew that. But she just didn't care. She was completely over Ainsley and her Gustare Foods' standard checks for every little freaking thing. She propped the door open with a spare crate, descended the stairs into the cellar, and began loading bottles needed to restock the bar, trying to shake off her annoyance. When it came to food, sometimes it was more important to follow your gut than a checklist. That's just the way it was. Her father knew that, and so did she. That's how they'd kept the place going all those years. She didn't need some big corporation to tell her otherwise.

She was still grousing when she heard the telltale creaking of the stairs indicating someone was coming down. *Fucking great.*

She kept her back to the door. Maybe if she ignored Ainsley she would just go away.

"I know you're angry, but at least let me help," Ainsley said. Her voice was softer than it had been when they were snapping at each other upstairs. When Gabi didn't respond, she went on. "I'll load up this crate."

Gabi didn't ask what crate she was talking about. She didn't care. She didn't want to pay Ainsley any attention at all, but when she heard the slam of the cellar door followed by the click of the latch, she whipped around. "What did you do?"

"I came down to help. We can each make a trip or two up to the bar instead of you making sev—"

"I meant the door," Gabi interrupted as she pushed past her to the door, but as she expected, it was caught and the knob wasn't engaging. They were trapped. She pressed her head dejectedly against the door, silently pleading for the knob to catch and the latch to magically release. This could not be happening. This was some worst-case scenario shit. "Fuck!"

"God." The empty crate Ainsley had been holding dropped to the floor. "If you're going to be so dramatic about it, I'll just leave you alone to do it yourself."

"You can't. Don't you get that?" It was all Gabi could do to not bang her head against the door. Was this woman's brain as empty as the crate she'd just dropped? What did she not understand about *you let the broken door shut*? "We're stuck in here. The latch on the door is broken and we keep that crate by the door to keep it from accidentally shutting. You moved the fucking crate."

Ainsley's expression morphed from annoyance to something more like horror. "I didn't mean to…I was just trying to…" She gulped in air and blinked fast like she was holding back tears.

Please don't fucking cry about it. The only thing worse than being trapped with Ainsley in the wine cellar would be being trapped with Ainsley in the wine cellar while she blubbered about it. She needed to take control of the situation and fast. Yelling and swearing about it was only pushing Ainsley over the edge and wasn't going to get them any less stuck anyway. "It's okay. We'll be fine."

"Do you have your phone?" Ainsley was still doing the rapid blinking thing, but at least her voice seemed steadier. "I left mine upstairs in my purse."

"I do, but it doesn't matter." Gabi shrugged. She turned to the hutch in the corner of the cellar and dug through the contents in the top drawer. "There's zero reception down here. No signal."

"Oh." There was the waver in her voice again. "Okay, so what are you looking for? Do you have a plan?"

"Yep," Gabi said triumphantly, holding up a corkscrew. "I plan to pop open one of these bottles and try to relax until the staff comes back in tomorrow morning and someone lets us out."

"Tomorrow morning?" Ainsley's jaw nearly hit the floor. For once she seemed to be rendered speechless.

"Yeah, so may as well get comfortable." Gabi continued to struggle with the cork. "We're in for the night."

"No." Ainsley shook her blond head, eyes wide and wild. "There's got to be some way out. Why aren't there any windows down here?"

"Um, because it's a cellar?" Duh. Her ears burned with angry heat, but Gabi focused her annoyance on the cork, and with one final pull, drew it out of the bottle.

"Don't use that tone with me. I'm trying to think outside the box and save us since you're too busy boozing it up to do anything."

"That's because there isn't anything to do since you locked us in for the fucking night." Gabi exploded. "No one knows we're down here, and no one is coming back to the restaurant until morning. So get over your delusion that there's some kind of *escape room* solution that will get us out of here. It's not gonna happen."

"*I* locked us in?" Redness crept up Ainsley's neck into her cheeks. "How long has that door latch been broken? Years? Did it never occur to you that a door that locks when it shuts behind you was a catastrophe waiting to happen?"

"Of course it did. That's why we kept the crate there."

"It's a fucking crate!" Ainsley snapped. "Not exactly a fail-safe plan. This is a perfect example of why you need help from Gustare Foods."

They were standing close enough for Gabi to feel the angry heat emanating from Ainsley. Ainsley stood there with her jaw squared and her chest puffed out just daring Gabi to challenge her. It made Gabi want to grab her and shake that smug look right off her face. Or grab her and kiss it off. *Wait, no. What the hell was that?* The first one, definitely. "The damned door can be the next thing you and Gustare Foods change since everything we do here is wrong and according to you, I'm not suited to managing a restaurant."

She hadn't meant to say it out loud. She hadn't meant to admit her fear to Ainsley. But something about the way her insides buzzed when she imagined that kiss made her need to push. It made her want to run away, but obviously that wasn't an option. And since putting hands on a coworker wouldn't help her prove she was capable of managing the restaurant, verbal pushes and shoves were all she had.

To her credit, Ainsley had the courtesy to at least look surprised. "I'm trying my best to help you through this transition."

She looked like she was being honest, or maybe she was just a damn good actor. *Ugh.* What difference did it make? Gustare Foods wasn't going away anytime soon.

Gabi took a swig of wine right out of the bottle and felt some of the tension in her shoulders melt away. She was going to be stuck in close quarters with this woman for hours and she didn't really want to spend all night fighting. She blew out a sigh of surrender and the fight-or-flight urge subsided some. "Whatever. Grab a couple of tasting glasses from the hutch and I'll pour you some wine."

"You blamed me for being stuck down here and now you want me to have a drink with you?"

"Well, you're the one who moved the crate, so it is your fault." Gabi gave a snarky snort. "Besides, it will give you a chance to blather on about Gustare Foods' best way to pour and sip red wine."

"You're being ridiculous." Ainsley rolled her eyes. So freaking dramatic. "I'm a consultant. Advising on best practice is what I do. Of course, now that you've got that idea in your head, you're not going to let it go because you're so damned stubborn."

"I'm ridiculous *and* stubborn?"

"That's right." Ainsley crossed her arms, defiantly standing by her words.

They were name-calling? Two could play that game. Gabi set the wine bottle down on the bar and took a step closer to Ainsley to prove she wasn't backing down. "Well, you're overly critical and anally retentive."

"You're bossy and you yell too much." Ainsley also stepped forward, bringing them even closer.

"You're infuriating." Gabi could smell the strawberry gloss on Ainsley's pink lips. "And sexy."

Ainsley's eyes went wide with surprise. "What?"

Crap. Did she say that out loud? "The cabernet. It's rich and sexy. I think you'll like it." She put some space between them and filled a glass for Ainsley before holding up her own. "A toast to the know-it-all of the dining room. Maybe the wine will loosen the stick up your ass."

Ainsley frowned at her but took the glass. "I see your *stick up the ass* and raise you a stuck in the past and unable to change."

"I'm stuck in the past? That's not what we're doing here at all. This is tradition. My pop has been doing things at D'Angelo's this way since he took over from Nonno in 1993. And I'm doing my best to follow in his footsteps. Anyway, that was supposed to be a toast, not a poker game."

Ainsley stared back at her as if to indicate she didn't need words to prove her point—Gabi had done it for her with the 1993 reference.

God, this woman was something else. D'Angelo's didn't need to change. They'd been holding strong at the restaurant with their family recipes for over fifty years. Pop grew up shadowing Nonno in the kitchen, then Gabi had done the same with him. Family tradition—it was a thing. A wonderful, precious thing. Maybe she should tell Ainsley to look it up in one of her handbooks. Instead, she took another swig of wine. Arguing with Ainsley was futile—she'd already determined that. What she needed at the moment was peace in the wine cellar. "Look, the way we've done things has worked all this time. If it ain't broke, don't fix it."

Ainsley's expression softened and she put a gentle hand on Gabi's upper arm. When she spoke this time, her voice was kinder. "No one is saying D'Angelo's is broken, Gabriella. I'm merely here to assist—to be part of a team with you and the rest of your staff. D'Angelo's is a great family restaurant and you've done a lot of things right, but it's time for a few updates. With just a couple tweaks here and there we could really rejuvenate the place. Keep D'Angelo's going for another fifty-plus years."

Gabi glanced down at the hand and Ainsley quietly pulled it away. The movement was the opposite of what Gabi wanted. She wanted Ainsley's hold on her to linger. There was something in the soft touch that had sent a wave of warmth through her. It had calmed her instantly and she hadn't wanted the connection to end.

She remembered her promise to her father—that she would give this crap with Gustare Foods a chance. Maybe she should start living up to her word. Maybe thinking of it as *crap* wasn't really in the spirit of that promise, and leaning into it was the only thing left to do if she wanted to survive this collaboration. She drained her glass in one long gulp, then refilled it, topping off Ainsley's while she was at it. Maybe the cab was getting to her. "I can hardly imagine myself still slinging pasta in another fifty-plus years. That would put me in my eighties."

"Oh, no. I'm sure you would want to retire by age eighty. Then you can travel or take up a hobby like rock climbing or swing dancing."

Gabi laughed. "One can only hope."

Was she actually relaxing around Ainsley Becker? That was…new. A quick peek at her phone revealed it was just slightly after eleven, which meant they still had about eight hours before there was any hope of someone finding them, and that was a best-case scenario. A little peace between them might go a long way in their current situation. Gabi had thought by this time she'd be home on her couch watching *Friends* reruns and nursing an IPA. Her night had been hijacked before she even completed the final walk-through of the restaurant.

Fuck. She nearly choked on her mouthful of wine. The final walk-through.

"Ainsley, did we leave anything on up there? I know the kitchen was shut down, but I didn't look in the server station or at anything in the dining room really."

"Relax. The front-of-house checklist was completed before the last server left." She started ticking items off on her fingers. "Coffee maker and burners were off, refrigerators set to forty degrees, register closed out. The lights are still on, but the door is locked. Bet you're not mad about my checklists now."

Her momentary panic ebbed away. "I suppose I can see where they come in handy." It was the best she could concede, but it was a step in the direction of trying harder to be agreeable with this whole thing. Baby steps were still steps. "For a second there I was picturing us trapped down here while a towering inferno blazed above us."

"I'm not sure you're grasping the meaning of 'towering' in that phrase."

"Okay, perhaps more of a boiler room, Freddy Kruger situation then."

Ainsley pressed her lips into a straight line and raised her eyebrows as if she was waiting for Gabi to do the math on something.

"What?" Gabi finally caved, her curiosity getting the best of her. "What's that face about?"

"It's about you. Your references for what is happening right now were things from the early eighties," Ainsley replied and her eyes honest to God sparkled with teasing mirth. "I'm starting to think you really are stuck in the past."

"Shut up."

As their eyes met, an understanding flashed between them that this time the banter was purely joking around, and they both burst out in laughter. A much-needed moment of total relief.

Gabi set her wine on the hutch to keep from spilling it and put a hand on her middle to steady herself. She brushed at the tears on her lashes and tried to remember the last time she'd laughed that hard. *Damn.* She really needed to get out more.

"Actually, a nice hot boiler room sounds good to me right about now," Ainsley said when she'd finally caught her breath. "It's chilly in here."

"Well, you know." Gabi shrugged. "It's a wine cellar." When Ainsley rolled her eyes at the glib response, Gabi continued, "It's around sixty-five degrees. If it was much warmer the wine would spoil."

But Ainsley was right, her short-sleeved knit top, totally appropriate for indoors in April most likely wasn't doing anything for her now. At least she had long pants instead of one of those little skirts she sometimes wore to work. Gabi had on jeans which helped, but her D'Angelo's T-shirt wasn't the warmest garment either. At least if she'd still been wearing an apron she could've wrapped it around her like a shawl.

A quick scan of the room for anything wearable came up empty, but then she was struck with a flash of inspiration. "Hold on. I have an idea." She pulled out an old basket from one of the lower doors of the hutch, acutely aware that Ainsley was peering over her shoulder.

"Do you think a picnic will warm us up? I guess I could go for a nosh. I ate dinner before the rush." Ainsley took a step backward to make room for Gabi to dig through the basket. "Instead of toasting me again, perhaps you can call me a shrew while giving the blessing before our meal."

"That's very funny, but there's nothing to eat in here." Gabi found what she was searching for and she pulled it out with a flourish. "But there is a tablecloth we've used for picnics, and it's large enough to cover us both like a—"

"A blanket!" Ainsley exclaimed like she'd won bingo at St. Ursula's. "You're a genius."

"It's about time you noticed." Gabi nodded in the direction of the couch in the far corner. It was old and a little musty from living in the cellar all these years, but at least it was somewhere to sit. Shall we take our wine and try to get cozy?"

"I guess it's that or a wine barrel, so let's do it."

Gabi grabbed the bottle of wine, and they settled in on the floral-print couch. It took a minute to get situated with the tablecloth wrapped and tucked around them for warmth. Since their makeshift blanket was a heavy-duty vinyl with a flocked backing, Gabi had high hopes that it would hold their body heat. If not, it was going to be a damn cold night.

"I'm not judging because I'm seriously grateful to have it," Ainsley said between sips of wine, "but why is this old couch even down here?"

"This old classic." Gabi patted the lumpy cushion. "It's been in the wine cellar since my nonno ran the place. He'd sleep down here anytime Nonna got mad at him. Not sure what he did before he had this."

"Your nonna made him sleep down here?" Ainsley pressed her fingertips to her lips as if she was trying to stifle her giggle. "You're kidding, right?"

"One hundred percent truth." Gabi held up three fingers in a Scout's honor salute. "Never test an Italian woman's anger."

"Damn, I won't."

"I mean, you have." Gabi considered the beautiful woman beside her. Ainsley looked fairly cozy as she sipped her wine. The two of them were pressed together side by side to take full advantage of their body heat. Now she could not only smell Ainsley's strawberry lip gloss—paired nicely with the cabernet on her breath—but her shampoo too. It was something floral and feminine. It brought to mind the morning after they'd slept together—how the scent of Ainsley's perfume had stayed with Gabi as she walked to work. Then with a sinking feeling she realized the fact that she could smell Ainsley's lip gloss and shampoo probably meant Ainsley could smell the kitchen on Gabi. Poor dear, she was most likely being assaulted by onions and garlic. Maybe the food smells had been overtaken by the bleach used to sanitize the food prep tables at the end of the day. She couldn't imagine one was better than the other. She resisted the urge to sniff her shirt—no sense drawing attention to her smelly self. "You've tested mine on more than one occasion."

"Oh, please." Ainsley rolled her eyes. "I tested you? Do you have any idea what it's like to work with you barking orders from behind the swinging doors? You've made no secret of how much you dislike me. Which was not at all the vibe I got from you that night we met and I went home with you."

Ainsley was bringing up their night of sex. Was she feeling the urge to reconnect in that way again too? Because that feeling was stirring inside Gabi in a powerful way.

"I don't dislike you," Gabi protested but her brain was already racing to come up with a good explanation for her behavior up to that point. "I..."

Gabi's floundering gaze met Ainsley's *don't bullshit me* one, and both women burst out in laughter.

"Okay. I admit you weren't my favorite person when you first arrived at D'Angelo's," Gabi said finally. "But you're kind of growing on me, I guess."

"You guess?" Ainsley repeated and the corners of mouth twitched teasingly upward.

"Yeah. Well, you have a bitching knowledge of restaurant health and safety codes, so there's that." She shrugged and bit back a laugh as Ainsley's jaw dropped with dramatic outrage.

"Health and safety code?" Ainsley squinted at her. "That's what you see as my best feature?"

She couldn't very well say, "you've got a rockin' bod and gorgeous, clear-blue-sea eyes I want to drown in." Or could she? She took another sip of wine to fortify her courage. "You have a beautiful smile too. I've actually thought that since the first night we met. Even before we...well, you know."

Ainsley took another drink too, swallowing down the information. "You think I have a beautiful smile?"

"I do." Gabi was on a roll. The more words that came out of her mouth, the braver she felt. "You're also a highly effective manager—a good leader."

"I was an only child and spent a lot of time lecturing and leading my ranks of stuffed animals. Mimicking my father, I suppose." Ainsley looked thoughtful, as if analyzing her past behavior. "All that practice must have paid off."

Only child. That tracked with what Gabi knew about sociology—only children tended to be achievement-oriented, and ambitious, and tended to have trouble compromising. All traits that fit Ainsley.

"Was your father in business management too?"

Ainsley shook her head. "He was in the military and expected the same discipline at home. He was very strict and formal, both with his ranks and with us."

This was the first time Ainsley had mentioned her family, and Gabi was intrigued. Ainsley's family life growing up sounded quite different from her own experience. While neither Pop nor Nonna would tolerate foolishness from teenaged Gabi, she would never describe their family as formal. The D'Angelo household had a much more comfortable, lived-in vibe. Similar to the old couch they were currently cuddled up on.

"His guidance served you well then," Gabi pointed out. "From what I've seen, you're very disciplined. Organized too. Did your leadership only apply to your stuffed animals, or did you have checklists for directing your school friends too?"

Something like sadness flashed in Ainsley's eyes. "I didn't have many school friends. We moved around too much for that. It was usually just me and my stuffies." She shifted a bit as if uncomfortable, but then tipped her head, perhaps regarding Gabi in a new light. "That's something I admire about you. You really seem to form warm, genuine relationships. When you're not barking orders at people, I mean. Everybody here loves you."

"Ah, that's just the way I was raised. Growing up in this neighborhood we were all connected. Helping one another out is just what we do, and it's just natural to get to know your neighbors when you're working together toward a common goal."

"But that's what I mean," Ainsley said, tugging the tablecloth up higher toward her chin. "There's such a cozy sense of community here. I never had that growing up. Or ever, really. We never stayed in one place long enough to get to know our neighbors when I was a kid. I was always the new girl treading lightly, trying to fit in. And even now Gustare Foods keeps relocating me to train folks or consult at different restaurants. I'm like a rolling stone. I'd never thought about it much before, but I think I'd prefer what you have here in Bloomfield."

Ainsley's wistful look tugged at Gabi's heart. Ainsley had been the new girl at D'Angelo's and Gabi had been hard on her. It must have been like those old days of being the odd kid out at a new school all over again. Gabi's stomach sank. She definitely could've been kinder this past week. She felt the urge to take her in her arms and comfort her—make it all better. She placed a gentle hand on Ainsley's cheek and lifted her chin so their eyes locked. "You're here now. You have it."

Ainsley brought her face closer to Gabi until their lips were almost touching. "Do I really?"

"Absolutely," Gabi whispered before closing the distance between them and kissing Ainsley with all the passion and heat that had been building in her.

Ainsley responded, pushing her tongue into Gabi's mouth. Suddenly, it was surprisingly warm under that tablecloth, as chilly as it was in the cellar.

When Ainsley grabbed Gabi's hand and placed it on her breast, she took it as a clear green light to proceed. She felt the fullness of Ainsley's breast and let out a moan when the nipple hardened at the touch. In a flurry, shirts were removed, bras were discarded, pants were unbuttoned and unzipped, giving access to the wanting bodies underneath them.

"God," Gabi gasped as Ainsley rolled on top of her and trailed kisses down her neck. The throbbing between her legs was growing with anticipation. "Yes."

Suddenly Ainsley's mouth was on her breasts, sucking, licking, teasing. Gabi tangled her hands in Ainsley's long hair, first to encourage the attention on her chest, but then to guide her lower.

"Is there something you want?" Ainsley asked, her voice throaty as she nipped at the curve of Gabi's hip bone.

"Don't tease," Gabi begged. "Put your mouth on me."

The heat of Ainsley's breath sent a shiver through Gabi's core, but when her lips finally made contact, she had to bite her bottom lip to keep from crying out. As she had their first night together, Ainsley proved to be quite skilled at the task at hand...or at mouth as the case may be. Ainsley sucked and licked until Gabi was bucking her hips wildly as she tipped over the edge and pleasure shot through her body, bubbling in her head, tingling in her fingertips, making her toes curl.

The moment she caught her breath Gabi twisted around to top Ainsley. She kissed her hard and forcefully on the lips and slid her hand down Ainsley's abdomen. Then lower. At Ainsley's lustful moan Gabi's center quaked—an aftershock of bliss tearing through her. She pushed one finger, then two, into Ainsley's wetness and rocked with her as she drew her closer to orgasm.

"Don't stop," Ainsley pleaded, gulping air.

Gabi had no intention of stopping until she brought Ainsley to the same pleasure she had experienced. "I want you to come for me."

And with a final yelp, she did.

Gabi slid off her but snuggled against Ainsley, draping an arm casually across her middle. "That was—"

"Awesome," Ainsley finished for her.

"Mmmm," Gabi agreed and planted a gentle kiss on her shoulder. But then a thump from somewhere above them caught her attention. "Did you hear something?"

"It's probably my heart," Ainsley sighed. "It's still pounding."

"Mine too." Gabi blew out a long breath, settling into the moment and joy she felt cuddled close with Ainsley. Her eyelids fluttered, and for a moment she thought she could drift into a peaceful sleep, despite being locked in a cold cellar. But the creaking steps quickly pulled Gabi out of her moment of afterglow.

Someone else was in the restaurant.

Based on her look of shock, Ainsley seemed to have the same realization. They both pulled away from the other to scramble for their discarded clothes just as the cellar door was yanked open. Luckily, the couch was in the far corner of the cellar out of the eyeline from the doorway, giving them a few extra seconds to get themselves together.

"What the hell happened in here?" Pop's booming voice as he entered the cellar held a tinge of laughter that Gabi didn't appreciate. Was it obvious what they'd been doing? "You lock yourself in, Gabi? Way to go, kid."

Gabi began folding their makeshift blanket, looking anywhere else but at Ainsley. What had she been thinking, having sex with her again. Talk about making an already difficult situation even more complicated. "Yeah, yeah. It's hilarious, Pop." Deflection was a good tactic. "Not that I'm not glad to see you, but what are you doing here anyway?"

"I was on my way home from Sal's and I noticed the lights were on. I got worried, so I stopped in. Good thing, huh? You would've been in for a chilly night. I thought there was a break-in or something. I never would've guessed I'd find you two down here."

Hopefully he hadn't guessed what they'd been doing down there either.

"It was actually my fault we got locked in," Ainsley confessed as she searched around the base of the couch, presumably for her shoes. Her blouse was untucked and wrinkled—a telltale sign of what had occurred only moments earlier. "I'm the one who moved the crate and let the door shut. I trapped the two of us in here."

"You know, I don't really want to talk about it. It doesn't matter whose fault it was. It was an accident," Gabi said as she shoved the tablecloth back into the hutch. She had to get them all out of the cellar before Pop asked any more questions. She took him by the elbow and steered him back to the doorway. "It's been a long night. And I'm sure we both just want to get out of here."

"You okay to lock up?" he asked, glancing over his shoulder one last time at Ainsley who was smoothing her hair back into place.

"Yeah," Gabi confirmed before inspiration struck. "In fact, why don't you walk Ainsley out and give her a ride back to her place. I'll straighten up down here and lock up."

Both her pop and Ainsley looked a little surprised but mumbled their agreement, wishing Gabi a good night before disappearing back up the stairs to the kitchen.

It felt like Gabi was holding her breath until she heard the back door of the restaurant shut confirming she was finally alone. She needed the quiet of the empty restaurant to take a minute and collect herself. It had been one thing when she'd slept with Ainsley before she knew about her assignment at D'Angelo's and the whole thing with Gustare Foods but doing so again now had not been the smartest move. She was supposed to be acting more professionally, not getting it on with the dining room manager in the wine cellar. And what if her pop had arrived just ten minutes earlier—what might have he walked in on? Embarrassment burned Gabi's cheeks. No, she would need to try harder to push it all down around Ainsley. No more mushy feelings about her, no more lusting, and certainly no more sex. Only professionalism from here on out, she promised herself as she took another swig of wine right out of the bottle, corked it, then she carried it and the dirty glasses up to the kitchen.

CHAPTER EIGHT

To Ainsley's surprise it wasn't the chill of the air in the wine cellar that roused her from slumber, rather the cold air coming in through her bedroom window which she'd left open just a crack. In her dreams she'd been nestled against Gabi's shoulder, snuggling together for warmth after they'd—

Oh my God. Talk about questionable decisions. She'd slept with Gabriella D'Angelo. *Again.* What had she been thinking? And why did she wish she was still in Gabi's arms instead of waking up in her bed alone? She'd probably broken about a dozen of Gustare Foods' rules the night before, yet she didn't even care. Sex with Gabi was just that damn good.

She yawned and stretched, her cold muscles waking up. It was her day off which meant she had the whole day to herself to do whatever she wanted. Or she had the whole day to sit around and wonder what Gabi was thinking about what had happened between them.

Surely it would go better than the last time they slept together, when the next day they discovered they would be working together with the difficult circumstance of an enormous power struggle. Gabi's weirdness that time was harsh, but understandable. Her shock of learning Gustare Foods was coming into D'Angelo's and that Ainsley would be leading the charge was obvious. Of course Gabi had felt awkward. This time was different. They'd had a week to get used to working together. Things between them had really improved since that first day.

But would Gabi call? Should Ainsley reach out to her? *Probably not.*

Okay, no. It was going to be a damned long day if she sat round torturing herself by trying to guess what Gabi was thinking. She needed to get out of the house. Perhaps even out of Bloomfield for the day.

* * *

An hour later Ainsley was dressed and ready to take the bus to a mall in the suburbs. A day of exploring and shopping was the perfect distraction. She found Ruby on the front porch watering the potted plants.

"Ainsley, where are you off to so bright-eyed and bushy-tailed?" Ruby gave her a toothy grin.

"Just off to do a little shopping. I'll be back later this afternoon."

"Good for you." Ruby nodded approvingly. "We're still on for dinner, right? I'm making a roast."

"Of course. Wouldn't miss it," Ainsley confirmed, and she meant it. She couldn't remember the last time she'd had a home-cooked meal, and she was really looking forward to it. "Do you need me to pick anything up for it while I'm out?"

"No, no. I have everything I need." Ruby looked her over. "There's something different about you today. Did you do your hair different or something, honey?"

Just a little healthy morning-after glow from getting it on with Gabi.

"Nope. Same old hairstyle."

"Well, there's something," Ruby insisted. "And whatever it is, it looks good on you."

"Thanks, Ruby." Ainsley practically skipped down the porch steps. "You know, it feels pretty good too."

* * *

When Monday morning came and went and Ainsley still hadn't heard from Gabi, she knew it wouldn't be a happily-ever-after situation when they finally crossed paths again. Sure, they'd both had a little too much wine, and yes, since they worked together, making out was probably not the best idea, but Ainsley sure couldn't say she hated it. Too bad it seemed like Gabi did.

After her day of retail therapy, Ainsley was ready to get back to Gustare Foods' business, and she was as prepared as she could be to face Gabi again. But she hadn't been able to scrub away the memory of their time together in the wine cellar. The encounter had been too hot and toe-curling to be shopped away. She couldn't imagine how Gabi was going to act as if nothing had happened, and yet based on their interaction since—or lack of it really—that was the play she was going with.

Ainsley was left feeling foolish about getting swept up in what had happened between them. Based on her silence, it was pretty clear Gabi had considered the sex an activity to kill time while they were stuck in the cellar, not an actual connection between them. And now they had to work together. *Great.*

Somehow they made it through all of lunch without being in the same space long enough to converse. Ainsley suspected Gabi was purposely avoiding her and the discussion they probably needed to have. So, figuring two could play that game, she kept herself busy, not even taking a break until the card-playing retirees came in.

"Hey, Vic. Hi, Ida. You're the first ones here," Ainsley greeted the couple as they came through the door. "I've got your table all set up for you."

"Hello, dear." Vic led his wife across the dining room. "I told you last week you didn't have to do that for us. We can handle a little table setup. We've been doing it for years."

Ainsley knew that was true, but she made sure the tables were pushed together and ready for the group. She wasn't taking any chances that one of their customers might get hurt moving furniture around. Besides, it was Gustare Foods' policy that only restaurant employees rearrange tables. Why expose the restaurant to unnecessary liabilities? "And I told you, it's my job to take care of our guests."

Gabi chose that moment to push through the swinging doors with the antipasto for the group. "And *I* told *you* these folks are more than guests, they're family."

Well, at least Gabi was speaking to her, although Ainsley didn't particularly care for the tone. She waited while Gabi delivered the plates and said hello to everyone, but then she followed her back into the kitchen.

Gabi didn't seem to notice or care. She ignored Ainsley's presence and went right back to her kitchen duties, lifting the lid from each of the big sauce pots on the stove and giving the contents a thorough stir.

The rich scent of tomato, basil, and garlic wafted through the kitchen, making Ainsley's mouth water, and for a moment she forgot she'd entered the kitchen on a mission. But enough was enough. They at least needed to talk about what happened the other night. Acknowledge it. Even if it had meant nothing to Gabi.

"Can I help you with something?" There was distinct annoyance in Gabi's question. She still didn't look up from her work. She just continued fidgeting with the pots on the stove.

How silly that Ainsley had thought they'd had some sort of breakthrough Saturday night just because they'd swapped a few personal stories and orgasms. Gabi was stubborn as ever.

"Are we going to talk about what happened the other night?" Ainsley's version of a loud whisper had an unfortunate desperate quality. It was panicky, even to her own ears.

Gabi threw a quick glance over her shoulder before responding, "I have no idea what you're talking about."

Why wasn't she surprised? Of course it had meant nothing to Gabi. She didn't even seem to remember it happened. And why did that fact make Ainsley's stomach sink a little?

"The sex," Ainsley whisper-hissed. "We had sex Saturday night when we were trapped in the wine cellar. Don't you think we should do something about it?"

Gabi finally offered up her full attention. "I *am* doing something about it. I'm pretending it never happened. And I strongly suggest you do the same because this is a place of business, not a dating app. We work together. We should be acting like professionals, not feeling each other up because we got a little tipsy. Where the hell are all your Gustare Foods rules for workplace decorum now?"

Oddly enough, Ainsley had been wondering the exact same thing. Apparently since their recent hookup, all her rules had gone right out the window, as evidenced by the way her insides fluttered when Gabi talked about feeling each other up. Sure. *Now* Gabi wanted to act professionally. Convenient. But probably—and Ainsley hated to admit it—the right thing to do. It was always tricky having a relationship with a work colleague. She knew that much from past experience. Ainsley felt her chest deflate as the realization set in. She was at D'Angelo's to do a job, and getting tangled up with the kitchen manager wasn't going to make it any easier. Not to mention it broke just about every Gustare Foods rule. "No, I…you're right. We'll just pretend it never happened and go on with our lives. We've got a restaurant to run."

"That's right." Gabi nodded. "You can go ahead and get back to your Gustare Foods agenda."

Ainsley blew out a frustrated breath. That same old song. Gabi sure knew how to make a girl want to forget a night of passion. "Message received. No more…fraternizing. I'll just stick to Gustare Foods' rules from here on out. All of them."

She turned to leave the kitchen, but Gabi stopped her with a hand on her shoulder. The familiar touch sent Ainsley's mind racing back to how they'd spent the night huddled up close together. Her exasperation dissipated. Just like that, she was a puddle of goo.

"I know you're a company gal. That's your thing," Gabi said. She tipped her head close, and although Ainsley's heart pounded in her ears, she could still hear the sincerity in her voice. "So, this is the best thing for you. For both of us. Just keep our relationship strictly professional and move forward. Really."

Ainsley still felt the sting of disappointment, but Gabi had made a good point—there was more to consider in this situation than just their feelings and amazing sex. Maybe strictly professional was all they were ever meant to be. Despite the heaviness in her chest, she gave Gabi an appeasing nod and returned to the dining room to get back to work.

CHAPTER NINE

Before the dinner rush started late Monday afternoon, Gabi sat at her father's desk—her desk—in the little office and stared at the bulletin board on the wall. All day Sunday, running errands for her nonna and cleaning her own house, she'd managed to distract herself from her thoughts and feelings. She had known being back at the restaurant working in the same space as Ainsley would make it hard to ignore the subject. But then Ainsley had cornered her and forced her to say something about it.

There were no two ways about it—they had to pretend that night in the wine cellar never happened, just like they had to forget about their first-night hookup. They had to keep their relationship purely professional. Still, she couldn't deny that, for her, it was something more than a couple glasses of wine that prompted that night in the cellar.

It still wasn't completely clear. One minute she'd been mad as hell at a ridiculous woman for locking them down there, the next they were snuggled up together and confiding in each other, and then it was like Gabi's whole being had been taken over by someone else. Her mind started blanking out the pushiness, the rule books, the Gustare Foods guidelines—everything about Ainsley that had made her want to scream. And her body had behaved even more appallingly. As soon as their bodies connected—even just side by side—under that stupid picnic blanket, it had been like a switch had flipped her to super-horny-teenager mode. It was all she could do to keep her hands off Ainsley's fit form, and it was some sort of miracle that she'd managed to summon the good sense to pull herself together when Pop made his way down the steps. Now she just had to deal with the memory of the way their lips had slid so easily against each other, and the heady feeling that strawberry lip gloss gave her. How their bodies moved perfectly together and how they each seemed to know instinctively just what the other needed to tip over the edge in ecstasy.

She hated that she had to be the voice of reason and shut down whatever may have been blooming between her and Ainsley, and she hated the look on Ainsley's face when she'd done so. But it was the only thing that made sense. Ainsley had to answer to Gustare Foods. Gustare Foods was trying to ruin Gabi's life. Shutting down the extracurriculars between them was the safest move. The smart choice for the both of them.

A knock on the office door saved her from wallowing in her thoughts any longer.

Danielle popped her head in. "Hey, I'm heading out. Paul's behind the bar for the night." She seemed to notice Gabi's lost gaze resting on the corkboard on the wall. "That's some old stuff pinned to that board. Now that you're in charge back here, are you going to give that a makeover?"

Gabi leaned back in the creaky, old wooden desk chair that had been there since Nonno was in charge. "This whole office could use a makeover, but I'm pretty sure it's not in our budget. According to Ainsley, our numbers are dangerously low, and our budget has no room to…wiggle, or whatever. Office renovation will have to wait." Gabi shook her head to ward off thoughts of Ainsley. No need to head down that path again.

"Geez. Not even a fresh coat of paint?" Danielle cringed and poked at an especially flaky patch of mint green on the wall.

Gabi blew out an overly dramatic sigh. "Maybe someday. For now I've got to figure out a way to meet Gustare Foods' expectations before they cut my budget altogether and Ainsley gets to manage this whole damn place."

Danielle hitched her hip up on the corner of the desk, suggesting she was settling in for a conversation. Gabi had a sinking feeling she knew why. "Gabs, you're not still on this anti-Ainsley thing, are you? Can't you just play nice while she's here?"

"You know how much this restaurant means to me. I can't just stand by and let some stranger come in and take over."

"Right. But she's not taking over, is she? She's just making a few tweaks—mainly in the dining room mind you—and all to make D'Angelo's the best it can be. Isn't that what she's here to do? Gabs, I love working here, but do I have to pick another paint chip off your office wall to prove a few upgrades around here wouldn't exactly be a horrible thing?"

"I know some things could use a little sprucing up, but D'Angelo's has something that a big corporation like Gustare Foods just doesn't understand—family tradition. We do things our way for a reason, and I don't need Ainsley butting in on that and trying to change everything. My heart wants to shatter into a million pieces every single time I walk into that dining room and see her making decisions I should be making and pushing all that Gustare Foods' mumbo jumbo on everyone."

Danielle rolled her eyes. "You are so dramatic when it comes to the subject of this woman. Why do you hate her so much?"

"I don't hate her," Gabi argued. She sure didn't hate her Saturday night when they were tangled up under that tablecloth. "But the way she walks around all confident and commanding, with her chest puffed out, and that pretty face forward like she owns the place, it just makes me want to—"

"Oh my God!" Danielle interrupted. "You just said, 'that pretty face.' You called Ainsley pretty! And when you mentioned her chest you kind of turned pink like maybe you were thinking a little *too* much about her chest. Getting all hot and heavy over there. You're into her. You want to get under the new management."

"I am so not into her," Gabi protested. "And I'm not even dignifying the last part of that with a response."

"Please." Danielle's knowing smile made Gabi's cheeks burn. "I've known you forever. I know this look on you, and exactly what the look means. So, try again."

Her bestie was going to drag it out of her anyway. Why prolong the agony? "Fine. It's a long story, but we got trapped down in the wine cellar Saturday night and we…did it."

"Holy crap!" Danielle stretched her leg out to kick the office door shut, giving them a bit of privacy. "Keep saying words."

"What?" Gabi shook her head. "There's nothing else to say. We were trapped in the cellar, we had too much wine, we got a little friendly."

"Oh, come on." Danielle tapped her foot like she was losing her patience. "*A little friendly*? Spill it."

"That's the truth," Gabi insisted. "It's not going to happen again. We were huddling together for warmth, and we had a couple glasses of wine. The next thing I knew we were kissing, and then…you know. It was a bad decision since we have to work together and since she works for Gustare Foods, which is basically the bane of my existence these days, so that's the end of it. Pretty much."

"Okay, I hear what you're saying about the working together thing, but what's the *pretty much* part about?"

Gabi shrugged. "I don't know. It kind of sucks because I like Ainsley personally, but I can't get involved with someone I work with. We're both here at the restaurant—together—all the time. It would be too weird."

"Is this really about not getting involved with someone you work with?" Danielle narrowed her eyes at Gabi. "Or is it about Hannah?"

"Why would this be about Hannah? I never worked with her."

"You know what I mean. The way you just lit up talking about Ainsley—you haven't looked like that since you were with Hannah." Danielle straightened a messy stack of kitchen-equipment catalogs on the desk next to her. Fidgeting, like maybe she was debating how hard to push. "You know, just because things ended badly for that relationship, doesn't mean that's how it will go next time. I've seen what you've been doing these past couple of years. You have fun—one-night stands or whatever—but you don't let anything stick. I think you're afraid, and that's what's happening here."

"That's what you think, Ms. Know-It-All?" Gabi laughed and rocked back in her chair. What did she expect? Her best friend really did know her better than anyone else. Still, Danielle wasn't seeing the whole picture. "Don't you think part of it could be the fact that Ainsley is here on behalf of Gustare Foods? How could I possibly continue to hook up—or anything else—with someone who is part of that? I'd be a total traitor to my family. Maybe when she's finished her job and gone…"

A beat of silence passed between them before Danielle surrendered and slid off the desk. "Okay, if that's the story you're sticking to I'll drop it. But if you change your mind and want to talk about your actual feelings, or your fear of catching them, I'll be here for it." She gave Gabi's shoulder a squeeze. "By the way, I came in here in the first place to remind you about my house party this weekend. If you can get out of here on time you probably won't miss much. Darrius probably won't even start until ten or ten thirty."

"I'm going to try my best to make it. I still can't believe your little brother is on the verge of being a household name."

"His *band* is on the verge of being a household name," Danielle corrected. "That kid's got a big enough head, don't make it worse."

Darrius had been a talented vocalist even when he was a kid in the church choir, but it wasn't until his band, Sweaty Yeti, had a mildly popular hit on TikTok the year before that he finally got his big break. Since then, Sweaty Yeti had signed with a major label.

"Their record drops in like two months and he's the front man," Gabi pointed out. "People are going to know his name. And trust me, I will say I knew him when."

"I know he's going to want to see you, so get your ass to the party." Danielle jabbed a well-manicured finger in Gabi's direction. "You should bring Ainsley with you. Get to know her outside of this place before you rule starting something with her out completely."

"What? Bring Ainsley to the party? No. I don't think so."

"Your face is pink again. I can tell you kind of want to." Danielle smirked. "Just think about it." She slipped out of the office before Gabi could protest further.

Take Ainsley to a function outside of work? That didn't seem very professional at all. No. Danielle could make all the jokes and throw all the knowing looks she wanted, but this was not a thing that was going to happen. Gabi spent plenty of time with Ainsley at the restaurant, and the memory of their close-quartered time in the cellar was haunting enough without tempting fate further.

From here on out it would be all business all the time.

* * *

As she had promised Danielle, as soon as the kitchen cleanup was completed the night of the party, Gabi locked up the restaurant and hurried the seven blocks to join the fun.

She heard the event from down the street, even before she could see Danielle's house. Strong bass thumping, electronic drumbeats, and the sound of gleeful voices—friends coming together, laughing and sharing, and generally making merry—guided her. A jolt of excitement shot through her as she walked around the house to the backyard. It had been a while since she'd let loose at a good old-fashioned house party. She quickly spotted Danielle and Darrius among the dancing crowd, and she made her way toward them.

"Look who finally arrived." Danielle greeted her with a hug.

"It's about time." Darrius pulled her in for a squeeze when his sister released her. Gabi remembered him as a toddler following her and Danielle around back when they were in high school. Seeing him now, a full grown—and rather hunky—adult, was a real mindblower.

"Sorry, I had to close up. I didn't miss your set, did I?"

"Nah, you didn't miss a thing. Sweaty Yeti goes on in about twenty minutes." Darrius flashed his bright smile at her. "By the way, you look fantastic, girl."

Still dressed in her D'Angelo's T-shirt and with her hair shoved back in a hastily styled messy bun, Gabi suspected Darrius may have been stretching the truth a little, but she appreciated the comment nonetheless. "Still quite the charmer, eh, Darrius?" She gave him a playful shove in the shoulder. "You on the other hand, look like an honest-to-God rock star."

It was true. In his leather pants, bleach-splattered Sweaty Yeti tee, and heavy eyeliner, Darrius had an ultra-chic style that screamed celebrity.

"That's because my baby brother *is* a rock star." Danielle beamed.

"Who, me?" Darrius preened and posed for a beat before cracking a smile again. "Nah. I'm just a guy who's glad to be back in the neighborhood for a minute."

"Speaking of the neighborhood, did you hear what Gabi is bringing back this year?" Danielle asked her brother. "The Slice of Italy Festival."

"It's not just me," Gabi quickly corrected her. "We have a whole committee working on it. But, yes, it's coming back."

"No way!" Darrius's face lit up. "I loved that festival. Leave it to my hometown hero to be the one to bring it back."

What did he call her? Gabi shook her head, maybe she had misheard with all the loud music. "Hometown hero? What are you talking about?"

Darrius expression shifted from cool dude to something much more soft and sincere. "Aw, you know, Gabi. I've always admired you. You were the first openly out person I knew. Just by living your truth you helped me feel like I fit in this world."

He tilted his head slightly but didn't break eye contact. "Back then I thought I was crushing on you, but it turned out to be more of a *be like you* than a *be with you* situation."

They all shared a laugh.

"Anyway," Darrius continued. "I'm forever grateful, and I mean that. If there's ever anything I can do for you, you know where to find me."

"Thanks, Darrius." Gabi's heart swelled. She'd never realized what an impact she'd had on the kid. She was just being herself—she didn't do it with any higher purpose in mind. But it warmed her to think that it helped someone else. "That's really sweet of you to say."

"Darrius!" They were interrupted by a beefy guy with a guitar slung over his shoulder yelling from the makeshift stage area. "It's time."

After Darrius excused himself, Gabi and Danielle left the dance floor to get a drink before Sweaty Yeti took the stage. On their way toward the beer keg, Gabi caught a glimpse of a familiar blond head near the front of the line.

Gabi grabbed Danielle to whisper loudly enough for her to hear, "What is Ainsley doing here? I didn't invite her."

"I knew you wouldn't." Danielle smirked. "So I did."

"You didn't." Gabi groaned, but before she could expand on her feelings about the situation, Ainsley spotted them.

"Hey, you're here." Ainsley raised her full red plastic cup of beer at Gabi in salute before turning to Danielle. "Awesome party. Thanks again for the invite."

"You're welcome." Danielle nodded. "The band is about to start. Want to find a good spot out there to watch and we'll join you once we grab some beers?"

"Sure thing," Ainsley confirmed before taking a sip to keep the beer from sloshing over as she walked off.

Minutes later, all three of them stood in front of the stage bopping along to Sweaty Yeti's opening song. Along with his strong voice, Darrius had a charismatic stage presence. Gabi had a hard time tearing her gaze away from him, but Ainsley's proximity as she shook and shimmied in time to the music did the trick. The way she was gyrating her hips in those tight jeans, with her hands thrown joyously in the air was absolutely mesmerizing.

"What's wrong with you?" Ainsley had a teasing lilt in her voice. "Too cool to dance?"

Gabi had been caught staring. She compensated by doing an exaggerated hip shake of her own. Taking Ainsley's words as an invitation, she moved close behind her so that they were close, although not quite touching. "I've got moves."

Ainsley took the slightest step backward, until she was pressed against Gabi, and their bodies rocked in unison for the rest of the Sweaty Yeti song.

While the crowd applauded, Gabi leaned forward and whispered, "That was fun, right?"

Ainsley spun so that they were standing nose to nose. "It was, but what happened to lying low and acting professional?"

"We're not at work now." Gabi shrugged. There was a total difference between getting it on in the wine cellar and some dirty dancing at a house party. Although, a quick glance at the crowd around them revealed at least a half dozen coworkers. She swallowed down the arousal building as they danced and took a step away from Ainsley. "But you're probably right. We should cool it."

The disappointment that washed over Ainsley's face made Gabi's heart sink, but it was the smart thing to do. Gabi quickly gulped down the last of the beer, giving her an excuse to escape the situation. She needed to cool off before she could act like she wasn't completely turned on and desperate to get Ainsley into bed again.

"Refill," she said simply before heading for the keg.

Be cool, be cool, be cool, she repeated in her mind in time with her footsteps as she walked away. But it was neither her mind nor her feet that needed to get the message.

CHAPTER TEN

To Ainsley, making it past the lunch rush on Sunday felt like crossing a finish line at the end of a marathon. It had been a busy week of work, and a smorgasbord of emotions where Gabi was concerned. It was exhausting. Every time Ainsley thought they were gaining some ground, they ended up being knocked backward a couple of steps. At Danielle's house party the weekend before, they had actually been having a good time together, but then suddenly it was like a switch was flipped in Gabi's brain and she went back into grump mode. Ainsley had survived at work by staying as far from the kitchen as possible. When lunch service was done and they were closing for the day, it was a relief to finally be heading out of the door that afternoon.

Only, she couldn't very well leave her apron lying in the server station when she had been reprimanding the servers for doing that exact thing all week.

It seemed Gabi spotted her the moment she stepped through the swinging doors. "Hey, haven't seen much of you lately."

"Just busy out front, I guess." Ainsley tried to avoid eye contact. Unload the apron and get the hell out of there. Do not get back on this merry-go-round.

But Gabi wasn't giving up. "Big plans for the evening?"

"Oh yeah," she said, tossing her apron into the bin. "Big plans with a can of soup and *Golden Girls* reruns on my tablet."

Something akin to horror flashed across Gabi's face. "You're eating something from a can for Sunday night dinner?"

"I mean, I'll heat it up first."

"No."

"Of course I will."

"No, not that." Gabi had her hands balled on her hips now, right back into kitchen boss mode. "I mean no, you're not doing that."

She was really something else. Was she telling her what she could or could not do after work now? Ainsley was too damn tired after hours on her feet to put up with someone disparaging her admittedly pathetic dinner plans. "Well, we're closed now and my shift is done, so I don't have to stick around and consider your opinions any longer. Thanks though, Gabi. Just pretend I'm on an extended break and find someone else to boss around in the meantime."

"Hey, no. That's not what I meant." Gabi's fingers closed around Ainsley's wrist, stopping her from making her dramatic exit. But when Ainsley turned around, Gabi quickly released her.

The jolt of excitement from that touch that shot through Ainsley seemed to short circuit her brain. She couldn't decide if she wanted to scream at Gabi for grabbing her or beg her to tell her what the hell she was talking about. On top of that, she was having trouble forming words because of the tingling in her core.

"Huh?" she finally managed.

"Sorry. I just…" Gabi held up her hands as if indicating she meant no harm. "I just couldn't believe that after being around all this delicious food all day you were going home to eat condensed soup. It's too sad."

"I didn't say 'condensed' soup." Ainsley found her voice again. "It's actually one of those hearty types you don't have to add water to."

"Still sad." Gabi shook her head, but her eyes twinkled with teasing. "How about instead you come have dinner with my family?"

It still felt like there was an insult in there somewhere, but was Gabi actually inviting her to her family dinner? Like, with her *and* her family? That was a lot.

The reason for her hesitation must have registered plainly on her face because Gabi continued, "Yes, it's with my family, but Pop made ricotta and spinach stuffed shells. Meatballs too." She wiggled her eyebrows suggestively. "And Nonna's homemade bread."

Ainsley's stomach growled traitorously. How could she possibly go home to her canned soup when she knew there were stuffed shells out there? "I don't want to impose."

"You're not. D'Angelo's family dinner is the reason we close the restaurant early every Sunday," Gabi said as she shrugged into her jacket. "Nonna loves to have more people at the table. And there's always enough food to feed the whole block. In fact, now that I've invited you it would be an insult to my entire family if you didn't come."

"Oh…"

"I'm kidding, Becker." Gabi laughed. "The choice is yours whether you want to eat a delicious meal or not. Grab your stuff. Let's go."

Decision made, they left D'Angelo's and walked the four blocks to the duplex that was home to Gabi's nonna on one side and Bruno D'Angelo on the other. It was Nonna's half that was hosting the meal.

The moment they stepped through the front door they were greeted by the mouth-watering aroma of garlic, butter, and fresh-out-of-the-oven bread. Ainsley's whole body immediately relaxed, the day's stress wiped away by the tangy scent of sauce simmering on the stove.

In the dining room, Gabi introduced her to her nonna, her aunt Mary Louise, and three cousins, David, Matteo, and Dominic. Everyone was already seated and passing a salad bowl around.

Gabi's cousins looked to be around the same age as her, late twenties to midthirties. All buff-shouldered guys with dimples accenting their amiable smiles. Maybe the D'Angelo charm all landed on that side of the family and missed Gabi altogether. That could explain why Gabi was so hot and cold with her. The boys also had the same thick, chocolate-brown hair as Gabi. Clearly an all-around family trait.

"Don't just stand there, Gabriella." Mary Louise's bright hot-pink glossed lips pursed with disappointment as she scolded her niece. She flicked a hand in her niece's direction, showing off a manicure that matched the same pink hue as her lipstick. "Get our guest a place setting. Honey, you sit right there next to Dominic."

Ainsley did as she was told, relieved when Gabi returned and took the seat on her other side. The D'Angelos were friendly enough, but they were loud and more than a little intimidating.

"Who needs some wine?" Sal's familiar voice boomed as he joined the group, a bottle of white in one hand and red in the other.

Ainsley knew Sal from when he'd brought in wine and hung around the bar area. He was a near carbon copy of his older brother, with the same slim build and olive complexion. His thinning hair still held a bit darker brown than Bruno's though. She gave him a little wave.

Bruno entered the room behind him with a pan of stuffed shells held up above his head like it was the victor's spoils. "I thought I heard Ainsley's voice. Benvenuto."

"Thank you." She accepted a generous pour of wine and gave Bruno a grateful smile before turning to Gabi's grandmother. "I appreciate you having me, Mrs. D'Angelo."

The whole table erupted with laughter and six different versions of "Call her Nonna!"

"Yes, dear." Nonna smiled kindly, her Italian accent beating out the Pittsburghese in her voice. Her gray hair was piled on the top of her head in an enormous bun that shook when she spoke. "Please, it's Nonna."

"Nonna," Ainsley repeated. She liked the way she felt when she said the word—like she was included in a special club. "Well, I'm really glad Gabi brought me here with her. She does a great job running the kitchen at D'Angelo's. I'm sure you're proud of her."

"Very proud. Gabriella is an excellent cook," Nonna proclaimed.

"I should be," Gabi said, beaming at her grandmother then her father in turn. "I learned from the best."

Ainsley's heart melted at how this family looked at one another. There was obviously so much love between them. She would've never thought that tough-talking kitchen manager would have such a soft side when it came to her nonna and pop. It was so sweet. And this gathering was completely unlike any family dinner she'd attended before.

"I believe it," Ainsley said, helping herself to another slice of garlic bread. "I've eaten a lot of delicious meals at the restaurant."

"At the restaurant?" Nonna looked taken aback. She clutched the gold cross on her necklace and narrowed her eyes at Gabi. "You haven't cooked this woman dinner yet, Gabriella?"

David let out a low whistle and Matteo tried to disguise a guffaw as a cough.

Nonna continued, "Gabriella loves to cook for the—"

"Yeah, yeah. I think cooking is my superpower. We got it, Nonna." Gabi, who had been growing increasingly fidgety before cutting her nonna off, removed the napkin from her lap and stood. "I...I'm going to grab another bottle of red," she mumbled by way of excusing herself from the table and hightailing it to the kitchen.

Left at the table where all eyes turned to her, Ainsley stood too. "I think I'll just go help her with that." She found Gabi in the kitchen, leaning against the counter and staring out the window at the dark backyard. Ainsley cleared her throat and Gabi turned to face her, scrubbing a hand over her face as if trying to pull herself together.

Ainsley put a gentle hand on her shoulder. "Are you okay? What was that about?"

"You have to excuse Nonna. She's very enthusiastic when it comes to my cooking. Anyway," Gabi said, grabbing a bottle of wine from the counter. "More red?"

"Hold on." Ainsley wasn't ready to let this go. Gabi was clearly bothered by something and if they went back into the dining room among the dinner din of the D'Angelos she'd never find out what it was. She wasn't accepting this back-and-forth act from her any longer. "What am I missing? One minute we were enjoying dinner with your family, the next you were hiding in here. What's going on with you?"

"Nothing. I'm fine." Gabi shook her head. "Let's go have more carbs. I'm sure my family will behave while we finish dinner."

"Behave? They've been perfectly lovely since I've been here." Things still weren't adding up. Was this not normally how the D'Angelos acted when they had guests for dinner? Unless… "Do you never bring people over for dinner? I knew I was intruding."

Gabi looked horrified. "Oh, God, no. Please, Danielle comes over to eat all the time. It's not that."

"Then what is it?" Ainsley pressed. "Why are you acting weird?"

The tapping of Gabi's finger against the wine bottle was the only sound in the kitchen. She swallowed hard and her expression softened as if she was entertaining an internal debate on how much to divulge. "It's awkward with Nonna bragging on me like that in front of you. It's…embarrassing."

"Embarrassed? You? The biggest ego in the kitchen?"

"Yeah, I know." Gabi shrugged and shifted her weight from side to side. She looked like she was anxious to change the subject.

There had to be a real reason. And the embarrassed thing was obviously bull crap. God, this woman was so damn stubborn. What was it that Nonna had said that set all this in motion? Something about *she loves to cook for the...what*? Suddenly the last piece of the puzzle clicked for her. "Ladies? Is that what your nonna was saying? That you love to cook for the ladies? To what? Impress them?" She bit back a laugh. "To...seduce them?"

"Come on." Gabi rolled her eyes.

"Wait a minute." The realization washed over Ainsley, and it made her jaw drop with shock. "Was your nonna saying that you...Do you want to seduce me?"

Suddenly Gabi's demeanor shifted back to a more familiar countenance. She flashed a wolf grin. "You want me to seduce you, sweetheart?" She took a step forward, closing the distance between them.

The heat that shone in Gabi's eyes caused a distinct throbbing between Ainsley's legs. "I, uh..."

Gabi's throaty laugh brought Ainsley back to reality. She was teasing. Of course. The old hot-and-cold routine.

"Oh, ha ha." Now it was Ainsley's turn to roll her eyes. There was the Gabi D'Angelo she knew and...well, not *that*. How could her mind go *there*? Anyway, it was good to be back on familiar ground.

"Seriously, do you want me to cook for you?"

"I..." The teasing was over, right? Or was she walking right into the next joke? Despite the warning bells, she just couldn't seem to resist Gabi D'Angelo. It would be worth it if saying yes earned her another one of those smiles—the kind that shot that jolt of excitement to Ainsley's nether regions. "I would like that."

"What are you doing tomorrow?"

"Working," Ainsley replied. "And so are you. We're both on for the dinner shift, remember?"

"Right. The dinner shift." Gabi nodded solemnly. "There are other meals besides dinner though. You eat lunch, right?"

Yep. More teasing. "I adore lunch." She could play along. "Great. I'll pick you up at nine."

"Nine seems a tad early for lunch."

"We're going to run a few errands first. And I'll ask Brian to cover my dinner prep tomorrow to give us a little extra time before we have to report to work." Gabi winked at her as she headed toward the dining room again. "Don't worry, I'll show you a good time."

That escalated quickly. Ainsley's heart skipped with excitement. A good time sounded…intriguing. Before she could overthink it, she heard herself say, "Nine it is then."

* * *

The two-block walk from their parking spot passed quickly as Ainsley enjoyed the bright morning sun on her face, but once they hit the stretch known in Pittsburgh as the Strip District, her jaw dropped in awe. It wasn't that it was anything fancy, just converted warehouses and weathered brick buildings. Old relics of yesteryear. But the buzz of energy in the air was outstanding. Despite it being early on a Monday morning, there were people of all ages and walks of life milling around. And most of them seemed just as excited as she was to explore the Strip's stores and street carts.

Ainsley took in the view up and down the block—old-style grocers, boutique stores, sandwich shops and bars. The rich aroma of roasted coffee and freshly baked bread wafted happily in the air. Across the street at a little cart an old man under a big black and gold umbrella was grilling veggies and chicken on a stick. Another delicious aroma mingling with the others. The place was foodie heaven.

Anticipation and delight hummed in Ainsley. Everything she was interested in trying came tumbling out all at once. "We should get some coffee and maybe something sweet to go with it from that bakery. And, oh my God, is that a penny-candy store? Do you think they have those little root beer barrels?"

Gabi laughed and linked their elbows, physically tethering them together to rein her in. "Don't worry, we'll check it all out, but one step at a time. We could start with coffee though."

They meandered along the sidewalk in silence for a moment before Gabi spoke again. "Now that you know about the Strip, you can come any time you want."

Ainsley's head continued to swivel left and right, trying to take it all in. Where would she even begin if she didn't have Gabi to lead her? It was too much for a newbie to navigate alone. She squeezed Gabi's arm. Her giddiness overriding her common sense. "I'm glad to have a local to guide me. I'm... happy to be here with you."

Gabi's expression first registered surprise that melted into what looked like pride. Hometown pride. That seemed to be a common feeling in Pittsburgh.

"Yeah." Gabi smiled at her and bumped their shoulders together playfully. "Me too."

"Wow, what's Penn Mac?" Ainsley tried to peer around the letters painted on the front window of the storefront as they walked by, but there was too much to take in while they were still moving.

"We'll come back once we've had our coffee." Gabi grinned at her. "Believe me, it's better to see it for yourself than have me describe it. We'll pick up our ingredients for lunch there. You're going to love it."

* * *

An hour later when they finally stepped out of Penn Mac with their arms full of packages and mouths watering in anticipation of lunch, Ainsley couldn't contain her glee any longer. "This is incredible!"

"It was the cheese counter that pushed you over the edge, right?" Gabi nodded. "I know."

"The cheese counter was awesome, but it wasn't just that."

She thought of the right words to describe what she was feeling. All the sights and flavors of the morning swirled around in her mind. Wheels of cheese bigger than her head. More fresh pasta than she knew existed. But it was all even more special because she had Gabi beside her. She stopped in her tracks as the realization hit her. The day was better because she was spending it with Gabi. *That was new.* Ainsley couldn't very well just blurt that out. She'd let her guard down around Gabi before and only been burned. And now that she'd stopped in the middle of the sidewalk to get herself together, Gabi was totally looking back at her like she was concerned about her well-being.

"Sorry," Ainsley finally said, falling back into step with Gabi. "What I was saying was, it wasn't just about the cheese counter, it was everything. This morning has been perfect. I've had such a wonderful time. Thank you for bringing me here."

"You're very welcome." While they waited for the light at the crosswalk, Gabi linked their arms again and smiled, her deep-brown eyes bright. "But our day's not over yet. Wait until you taste my spaghetti carbonara. You're gonna love it."

Ainsley looked up and caught her eye just in time to notice a blush rising in Gabi's cheeks. Electricity crackled between them. Was it possible she was enjoying their togetherness just as much as she was? Would this time finally be different? The traffic light changed and the crowd around them began to move across the street. The spell was broken for the moment, but Gabi was right—they still had all of lunch ahead of them.

"I'm sure I will."

CHAPTER ELEVEN

Gabi led Ainsley through her living room to the kitchen where they set their packages on the center island. The afternoon sun streamed through the big windows at the back of the house, offering plenty of natural light and making Gabi grateful that she'd thought to give the kitchen a good scrubbing the night before. The last thing she needed was Ainsley pointing out health-code violations in her home. The thought of it made Gabi want to laugh, but she suppressed the smile she could feel playing at her lips.

The know-it-all kitchen-inspector side of Ainsley had been remarkably absent all morning. No criticisms, no looking for problems, no checklists. In a refreshing turn of events, all that had been replaced by a much more curious and wonder-filled Ainsley. A version Gabi had found quite charming and... attractive.

Not that Ainsley wasn't always attractive, but at work she usually dressed sharply in professional outfits, and she'd been wearing her hair neatly pulled back in a bun since that first day on the job when Gabi had scolded her. With her creamy complexion and long, blond waves flowing freely she'd turned a lot of heads that morning. Today's ripped jeans that fit her toned ass like a glove and simple white, nearly sheer V-neck tee was a revelation. Apparently, Ainsley was still capable of letting loose outside the workplace. While they were out and about she'd covered the outfit with a light cardigan that had a shaggy fringe, hip look. Now that they were in Gabi's kitchen, she'd let the cardigan drop from her shoulders before removing it altogether and draping it over one of the high-backed stools at the island. Gabi had a hard time refraining from staring at just how nearly sheer that white shirt was.

"How can I help?" Ainsley asked as she unloaded items from one of the cloth grocery bags. As she reached, her T-shirt pulled up enough to reveal a peek at her tanned abs.

Gabi was beginning to second-guess her choice to wear a sweatshirt. It had paired nicely with her cargo shorts for a morning of shopping in the Strip, but suddenly it was feeling mighty warm in the kitchen—and she hadn't even started cooking.

"If you could keep unpacking that stuff—get cold items into the fridge—that would be great," Gabi said as she grabbed a large pot from the cabinet on the far side of the room. "I'll get the water boiling for the pasta. It will take a while to get rolling."

"I can't wait to taste that spaghetti. I've never bought it fresh and by the nest like that."

"Are you serious?" Gabi stopped salting the pot of water long enough to turn and fix Ainsley with a questioning look. "You really don't get out much, do you?"

Ainsley scooted by her with an armful of colorful arugula to chop for their salad, bumping her hips against Gabi's as she passed. "Well, then I guess I'm lucky I met you." Her tongue darted out to moisten her bottom lip at just that moment.

Gabi's kitchen wasn't huge—especially compared to some of the commercial kitchens she'd worked in, but it was big enough that they didn't need to bump into each other as they maneuvered around the center island workspace. That had been a purposeful collision. She was starting to feel like she was the lucky one.

Gabi kept her gaze locked on Ainsley's as she reached into a drawer for a big spoon. "Well, you know—ouch!" So much for the sexy comeback. She looked down at the cut on her finger. Something in the drawer had caused a clean slice in the tip of her middle finger and beads of blood were already rising in its wake.

Oh no.

Her surroundings seemed to sway, and she inhaled deeply, trying to stay steady on her feet.

"Whoa, what's happening over here?" Suddenly Ainsley was by her side, guiding her gently down to the floor. "Just sit a moment. Right here."

"Sorry," Gabi murmured. "It's the blood."

"Oh!" Ainsley exclaimed, jumping up to grab a paper towel to press into Gabi's hand. "Hold this tight and breathe."

Gabi did as instructed and tried not to think about the throbbing in her fingertip. "I'm okay. It's just—" A nervous laugh bubbled out of her, embarrassed that Ainsley was witnessing her Achilles' heel. "It's so silly. The sight of blood makes me woozy."

"It's fine. Let me take a look at it." Ainsley took her hand and gently pried open her fist. Gabi kept her gaze averted, but Ainsley's reassuring hums indicated it probably wasn't a 911 situation. "Oh, Gabi, this isn't bad at all. The bleeding has pretty much stopped. What did you cut it on?"

"I don't know. Something in that drawer got me."

"Well, it cut you fairly cleanly and it's not that deep. We'll get you a bandage and you'll be fine."

Gabi frowned as she noticed the bright red streak on the front of Ainsley's shirt. "I bled on you."

"Don't worry about that. It will soak right out." Ainsley pressed her fist closed around the paper towel again. "Of course, you should probably sanitize everything in that drawer too, since something in there broke the skin and may have your blood on it."

Ah. There was the kitchen-health-and-safety side of Ainsley again. Somehow that was…comforting in this instance. Gabi was certain it was Ainsley's care that had stopped her dizziness, but she still moved slowly as she got back to her feet. "There's some in that skinny drawer there on the end. I'll grab you a fresh shirt." When she returned with an old but clean Pittsburgh Pirates T-shirt, Ainsley helped her get the Band-Aid around her finger.

Ainsley quickly changed her shirt right there in the kitchen. "I would've never guessed something like a little blood would make you woozy. You're usually so *large and in charge*."

That last bit sounded like it was supposed to be a compliment, but it could also be a euphemism for *really fucking bossy*.

She raised a questioning eyebrow that drew a giggle from Ainsley, who waved a dismissive hand. "You know what I mean. "It doesn't seem like anything fazes you at work. You really hold it down."

"You hold it down out front. I'm just *large and in charge* in the kitchen." Gabi couldn't keep the wry tone out of her voice.

"Are you kidding me? With the way I've seen you run things in the kitchen, I have no doubt you could manage that whole place. And I'm sure your dad would say the same."

"Eh." The subject of her pop limiting her management responsibilities to the back of the house coming up still felt like a blister rubbing against new boots. Sensitive and irritated. She could crack a joke and slide away from the topic. Simply change the subject. Or she could be honest with this woman who had just taken such good care of her. She took a deep breath and said it. "Actually, I have a pretty good idea why Pop questioned my ability to take over when he retired."

"A pretty good idea?" Ainsley stopped tearing the lettuce and stared at Gabi expectantly. Attentively.

Gabi sighed. "A very good idea." In for a penny, in for a pound, as Nonna would say. "I kinda got into it with an ex-girlfriend in the dining room a while back."

"Ouch. That sounds…cringy."

"Exactly." Gabi's ears burned just talking about it even after all this time. Two years and no love lost for Hannah, but the stench of the embarrassment from that day still stuck to her. "It wasn't my finest hour, that's for sure." To avoid eye contact she busied herself lifting the lid on the pasta pot to check if the water was boiling.

Ainsley went back to fussing with the salad greens, but Gabi could tell she was waiting for her to continue with the story. Just giving her the space to get there.

"She was cheating on me, and I didn't know it. Until she brought the other woman into D'Angelo's for lunch and to let me know she was breaking up with me." Gabi sighed. It was weird to say it out loud. Danielle had been there when it happened, so she hadn't had to relay the story to her. Of course, so was her pop. "It was just so humiliating for her to come into my place of work—my family's business—and break up with me there. In front of her new girlfriend too. I lost it. I told them both exactly what I thought of them, in many colorful terms. I said things that would make the guys in the kitchen blush. Lost it right there in the dining room. Not that they didn't deserve it, but I shouldn't have lost my temper like that at work. I know that. And I guess now I'm paying the price for it."

"Oh, Gabi. That's terrible." Ainsley paused her salad prep and gave her a sympathetic look. "She did you dirty, that's for sure. I'm sorry. I've had an ugly breakup before. They can be… rough."

Gabi shrugged hopelessly and pushed the pancetta around in the skillet. "It's in the past. Nothing to do about it now."

"You're right." Ainsley nodded and finished dressing the salad. "And you're wrong."

"What?" Gabi laughed. She moved the pancetta from the pan to a paper-towel-lined plate and dropped a nest of pasta into the boiling water. "How can I be both?"

"You're right that it's in the past. But you're wrong about the rest. You can do something, and I believe you are. You just said you are aware you could've handled things better that day, and I think that knowing that is truly half the battle." She put a soft hand on Gabi's shoulder. "You've learned from it, and you'll do better moving forward."

Warmth buzzed through Gabi's body at Ainsley's touch as well as the sentiment behind her words—Ainsley's confidence in her ability to change. It somehow bolstered her and made her want to do better. Despite Gabi's efforts to resist it, this woman had some kind of spell over her. Maybe she should give in to changing her feelings for Ainsley as well. "I hope I do," she agreed.

While Ainsley set the table, Gabi finished preparing the spaghetti, and finally they sat to share the meal. A happy moan escaped Ainsley as she took her first bite and Gabi's chest filled with pride.

"This is incredible," Ainsley said around a mouthful of pasta. "I could eat only this for the rest of my life and be happy."

"Your body might have some adverse feelings about that decision." Gabi laughed. "But thank you for the compliment."

As they ate, they talked about some of Gabi's other favorite home-cooked dishes, which led to a startling revelation from Ainsley. "I don't really have favorite home-cooked foods," she confessed. "Well, until now. Spaghetti carbonara is officially it."

"Hold on." Gabi placed her fork on her plate. "You really didn't have a favorite before this? How can this be?"

"Neither of my parents really cooked much, and I didn't grow up with grandparents to pass family recipes down to me. My family ate a lot of takeout and quick-prep meals. And we ate at a lot of restaurants, which is probably why I was drawn to my line of work. I've felt like a connoisseur of dining out since I was a child."

Gabi considered that as they carried their empty plates to the sink. It made her feel sad to think Ainsley had grown up without family food traditions. They had always been so important to Gabi and she couldn't imagine life without them. On a whim she pulled Ainsley into her arms. "I'm glad I've been able to share some of my family's love of food with you."

"Me too." Ainsley's warm breath tickled Gabi's lips. "Thank you for the delicious meal."

"You're welcome." Gabi's reply was an autopilot one. Her mind was focused on the way Ainsley sucked her bottom lip between her teeth after speaking, as if her mouth was just begging to be kissed. In one quick movement she closed the space between them and pressed their lips together, eliciting another moan of pleasure from Ainsley.

When the kiss finally broke, Ainsley whispered, "Take me to your bed."

* * *

Ainsley's head dropped back against the pillow, and she let out a satisfied breath. "God, that was amazing."

Between the way Ainsley had screamed out in pleasure while Gabi licked and sucked and pushed her over the edge, and the mind-blowing orgasm she'd experienced herself, Gabi agreed wholeheartedly—it had all been nothing short of amazing.

"Better than the carbonara?" Gabi teased. She eased herself onto the pillow beside her and ran a finger along the curve of Ainsley's hip.

"Are you asking me to choose between sex and food? I don't think I could."

"Me neither," Gabi mused. She was surprised—previously she would have said food, a no-brainer. But sex with Ainsley made the choice much harder.

"Ugh," Ainsley growled, suddenly covering her face with her hands like she was hiding from something.

"It was just a joke. You don't really have to choose." Gabi tried to reassure her.

"It's not that. It's just...ugh."

"Ugh is not the kind of comment I want a woman to make after sex with me," Gabi said. What changed in the last two minutes since they were both panting with pleasure? "What's going on?"

Ainsley reluctantly dropped her hands and rolled on her side toward Gabi. "I told myself I wouldn't let this"—she wagged a finger back and forth between them—"happen again. But here we are."

Gabi's stomach sunk and she pulled the sheets more tightly around her. Had she misunderstood something? "It was your idea to come to my bed. Did you really not want this to happen?"

"Oh no. I totally wanted this to happen," Ainsley quickly corrected herself. "And I'm very happy it did."

"And yet, you said, 'ugh.'"

A sad look that made Gabi's heart want to break crossed Ainsley's face. "The sex with you is always fabulous. I find myself on cloud nine afterward every time," she said slowly as if carefully selecting words. "But then afterward there's always an awkward distance between us. Not immediately, but later. Like the day we worked together after we were trapped in the wine cellar together. The sex—even though it was on an old couch in a cold cellar—was awesome. I left that night feeling great. But when I saw you at work on Monday, you were distant and told me to pretend like it never happened. The bubble had burst. And that part does not feel so great. In fact, it sucks. As great as I feel right now, I know what's coming. So, I'm bracing myself for the fall."

The fall? She didn't want Ainsley to fall. She wanted the exact opposite of that—she wanted to protect her from the fall. "Ainsley, I'm so sorry I let you down and caused you to feel that way," Gabi began. How could she explain that she hadn't meant to make things harder for either of them? "The only reason I was so insistent that we pretend it never happened was because I was trying to keep things professional. I didn't want our having sex to make things weird for us when we were working together. And now I see that the harder I tried to do that, the worse I made it. Geez, I'm sorry. This"—she mimicked Ainsley's gesture of pointing between them—"is very, *very* good. And besides the sex, I really like you."

Finally, a smile returned to Ainsley's lips. "I really like you too."

"It's settled then," Gabi proclaimed. "We like each other."

"We do," Ainsley agreed. But then her smile faltered. "But I'll only be here for a couple more months, so we shouldn't get too attached. My assignment in Bloomfield isn't permanent, you know."

Gabi knew all too well, although her perspective on it had certainly changed in the past couple of weeks. "We've finally admitted we like each other. We should at least explore that a little more. We'll make the most of our time together while it lasts," she promised before planting a sweet kiss on Ainsley's mouth.

Maybe that time will lead to something more, she thought but didn't dare speak it out loud. One step at a time was all they could do. And at the moment, the next step was the dinner shift at D'Angelo's. "I guess we better get to work. The restaurant's not going to run itself, you know."

"Duty calls," Ainsley concurred and slid out of Gabi's arms.

Although she knew they had to leave the bed, Gabi immediately missed the warmth of Ainsley pressed against her. *One step at a time.*

CHAPTER TWELVE

In the past week and a half since they had agreed to make the most of their time left together, Ainsley and Gabi had done exactly that. In addition to spending several after-work evenings together, they had also continued to explore Pittsburgh when their time off from the restaurant coincided with Gabi acting as tour guide while sharing her local pride.

They'd visited the Pittsburgh Zoo, where Ainsley had been absolutely thrilled to witness a penguin parade. She'd also been thoroughly charmed by the playful sea lions who seemed to be putting on a show especially for them, diving and darting around their pool. They'd also taken the T, Pittsburgh's light rail system to the Northside where they enjoyed ice balls purchased from a cart in the park, a treat Gabi had assured her was a Pittsburgh tradition.

They had a picnic at Point State Park, the large green space where the three rivers came together. That park was also home of the Fort Pitt Museum, but instead of engaging with history, they had settled in on a blanket near the fountain to eat lunch before Ainsley had to be at D'Angelo's for the dinner shift.

A light breeze blowing off the water provided cooling bursts of relief from the noonday sun. It was the kind of day where the sunshine on the grass made the whole world smell like summer, hopefully not far off. Ainsley inhaled the fresh air as she reached for another of Gabi's rosemary focaccia squares, one of her many tasty finger foods.

"I can't believe you made this," Ainsley gushed. "It's divine."

Gabi laughed. "Please, it's just picnic food."

"Well, it's delicious. Your dad really taught you how to do all of this? I mean, focaccia I get, but are you telling me the Asian slaw salad and the hummus are also your Italian family's recipes?"

"I picked some things up along the way." Gabi shrugged. "A lot of it I learned from culinary school. But don't get me wrong—my family gave me the foundation for all my favorite dishes, and they instilled in me a love of cooking that you can't be taught in school. I wouldn't be good at any of this without them."

"Culinary school?" This was news to Ainsley. She lowered her body and spread out on the blanket, resting her chin on Gabi's lap. Settling in for a conversation. "I had no idea you went to culinary school. Was it right after you graduated from high school?"

"No." Gabi lazily dragged a carrot stick through the hummus. "After high school I went to college and got a degree in business management."

Ainsley raised her eyebrows in surprise at her.

"What?" Gabi frowned.

"Nothing. It's just that *you* could have been the Business Management Barbie just as easily as me."

A guilty grin appeared on Gabi's face. "Well, you have the blond hair," she explained, shaking her brown curls as if to emphasize her point. "Anyway, I thought that was what I needed—like it made me more a more well-rounded individual to prepare to run the family business. But back then, Pop was nowhere near ready to retire, and I got itchy waiting. I thought that if I went to culinary school, got some experience in the real world outside of Bloomfield, maybe I could strike out on my own."

"Ambitious and headstrong," Ainsley commented and trailed her finger across Gabi's thigh along the hem of her shorts. "That tracks with what I know about you."

"Too headstrong for my own good." Gabi laughed. "I loved school, and I was pretty good at it too. But right out of school I was placed in an upscale restaurant in New York City called Optime. I worked there for almost two years, but it just...it never clicked for me."

"Life in the Big Apple isn't for everyone."

"There's a lot happening in that city for sure. But it wasn't just that." Gabi toyed with her necklace, sliding the small gold heart-shaped charm along the chain. It had belonged to her mother. She wore it whenever she wasn't working in the kitchen at the restaurant, where jewelry of any kind was frowned upon. She'd told Ainsley it was a reminder that her mother was always watching over her. Gabi was only three when her mother died of breast cancer.

"The whole time I was there, all I wanted was to be back here. Working at D'Angelo's. I'd have traded all of the fancy caviar blinis and truffle fries in the world to be back here in the 'Burgh slinging pizzas. I just couldn't hack it, I guess."

Hearing Gabi say anything that indicated she was less than one hundred percent confident unnerved Ainsley, but the way her expression had clouded kept her from asking any more about New York. Instead, she stuck with more familiar ground. "After that, you came back to Pittsburgh?"

Gabi nodded but remained silent, and for a moment Ainsley feared the mood of the entire date had been darkened, but suddenly she seemed to snap out of her reverie.

"Anyway, that's my story." She bent down to kiss Ainsley sweetly on the forehead. "And, if you want more of these delicious taste treats, come back to my house with me tonight after work. There are plenty of leftovers. And I can probably rustle up a cold beer or two to go with them."

"Leftovers *and* cold beer?" Ainsley laughed as she pulled Gabi down for another kiss—this time a lingering one on the lips. "How can I possibly resist?"

CHAPTER THIRTEEN

After they returned from their shopping trip and the groceries were all put away, Nonna found a few additional tasks around the house for her to tackle. Gabi didn't mind helping out on her morning off. That's what family did. When Gabi's mom died, the whole family had helped her pop raise her, but especially Nonna. The two had always shared a special bond. Whether it was forcing Gabi to sit at the kitchen table until homework was done or teaching her the family recipes passed down for generations, her nonna was a strong influence during Gabi's formative years. And her nonna remained the person she respected more than any other. Nonna had done so much for her, it was a debt she could never repay no matter how many light bulbs she changed or bags of trash she carried to the curb.

She had just finished breaking down some boxes for recycling when Uncle Sal came into the kitchen through the back door, consternation on his rugged face.

"What's wrong with you, Sal?" Nonna asked. She was sitting at the kitchen table, a week's worth of coupon fliers from the newspaper spread in front of her as she clipped away. "Do you need a cold drink?"

"I need something stronger than what you have in here, Ma," he replied, helping himself to a ginger ale out of the fridge. "Russo's canceled their standing wine order, so I went over there this morning to see what was going on. Damnedest thing. No Joey, no Nicky. No Russos there at all."

"What are you talking about?" Gabi's stomach squeezed uncomfortably. She abandoned her task and joined them at the kitchen table. She had to have misheard. Russo's had been around forever. "Are you sure?"

"Sure, I'm sure. You think I don't know my customers?" Sal groused.

Nonna smacked his hand. "You're upset. Don't take it out on Gabriella." She turned to Gabi. "And don't you ask silly questions."

"It just doesn't make any sense." Gabi was whining, but she didn't deserve the admonishment from Nonna just because Uncle Sal was harshing the vibe in the kitchen. "I mean, I know Nicky Russo was struggling to hold it down after his uncle retired, but that's why they brought in Gustare Foods." And *that* was the whole reason Pop signed the contract with them as well.

"Well, it still says 'Russo's' on the sign out front and on the menus, but Russo's it ain't," Sal said between sips of pop. "I didn't recognize a soul in there."

Nicky had brought Gustare Foods in to help when he took over the restaurant, and now the restaurant was still there but Nicky was gone. Something wasn't adding up. What the hell did Gustare Foods do to Russo's? She pushed her chair back to stand, nearly tipping it over in the process. "I've got to make a few calls. Sorry, Nonna, I've got to run."

"Don't worry about me, nipotina." Nonna waved a hand in the air, dismissing her. "Sal can help me finish up here."

Sal raised his can of ginger ale in salute.

"Love you both," Gabi said before rushing out the door.

* * *

Gabi had entered D'Angelo's through the back and gone directly to her office. Doing her best to avoid contact with anyone. She was on a mission. Her first order of business: call Nicky and get to the bottom of what happened over at Russo's. He was more than willing to explain.

"I was no good at running the place," he said simply. "When I heard about Gustare Foods, I figured it was the perfect solution. Russo's would keep going, and I could cash out. Win-win."

"Hold on." She tried to make sense of his words, *cash out?* "Didn't you bring Gustare Foods in to help you through the transition after your uncle retired?"

"Nah. That was just what we told people so they wouldn't know the restaurant would be under new management. It's part of the Gustare Foods agreement."

It still wasn't completely adding up for Gabi. "Nicky, I'm going to need you to back it up a little further. What exactly is it that you agreed to with Gustare Foods?" Silence stretched over the line, so Gabi pushed, "Nicky, I need you to be straight with me. My pop signed a contract with them too, and I'm starting to think he's getting more than he bargained for, or rather, *they're* getting more than he bargained for."

"Look, the nondisclosure clause in the contract forbids me from telling others about the arrangement." He blew out a surrendering sigh. "But I guess since your dad signed one too, he would know anyway. Gustare Foods comes in, works with you for a few months to make sure the staff is up to speed with their standards of operation and to keep up appearances with the public while the transfer happens, then they buy you out and take over the restaurant. They keep the place running with the look of a local mom-and-pop place, but it's actually a big corporation who owns it. That's their thing. That's why I told people they were just helping with the transition after Uncle Joey retired. It was like my cover story."

"Buy you out?" Gabi's mind reeled to take it all in. Pop had agreed to sell D'Angelo's?

"Yeah. Really fair price," Nicky confirmed. "I couldn't pass it up."

"And you told my pop all this?"

"Well, no. I told him the thing Gustare Foods wanted me to tell people—that they were helping me with the transition taking over for my uncle. I didn't mean to mislead him. I was just trying to hold up my end of the agreement. Part of the contract stipulates that if I do anything to publicize the restaurant is under new management, a monetary penalty will be applied. Basically, my sale price would be reduced. Not to mention, Gustare could take me to court for breach of contract. So, I totally tried to keep it on the down-low. I'm really sorry, Gabi. Is there anything I can do to help?"

"No. I...I don't think so. Thanks, Nicky," Gabi managed before clicking off the call.

Pop had signed an agreement with Gustare Foods to sell them D'Angelo's? Her stomach twisted. That couldn't be true. She had to read the contract for herself.

For once her father's old-school way of preferring paper over electronics had paid off—the contract had been easily found tucked in a manila folder plainly labeled "Gustare Foods" in the top drawer of the creaky, old metal filing cabinet. Unfortunately, what she read confirmed her fears—everything Nicky had told her was true. Pop had signed an agreement to sell.

Fucking hell.

She ignored the knock on the office door. She wasn't even supposed to be there—she wasn't technically working. Gabi needed to wrap her mind around why on Earth her father had put her in this position and why he hadn't been honest with her about his agreement with Gustare Foods. They'd never kept secrets before. As long as Gabi had been back working at D'Angelo's they'd been a team, running the business together. No secrets.

At the second knock, Gabi growled, "No one's in here. Go away."

Surely Pop had read the contract thoroughly before signing, right? There was no way he just took Nicky's word about what Gustare Foods was doing over at Russo's, right? Or was this another one of those situations where Pop didn't bother with the details and just heard what he wanted to?

The third knock pushed something inside Gabi to snap. She yanked it open to find Ainsley blinking rapidly, apparently taken aback by the force with which the door finally opened, and also looking kind of sexy in slim-fit black pants with a matching jacket over a pale-blue camisole. Gabi drew in a sharp breath. Ainsley was Gustare Foods, and Gustare Foods was about to be the new owner of D'Angelo's. Nothing about *that* was sexy. "What the hell do you want?"

"It's just…" More blinking while she tapped her fingertips together as if internally debating whether to go on or cut bait and run. "It's Friday and you're here already. Early for your shift. You're early and I wondered if everything was okay."

"It's my restaurant." *For a couple more months*, Gabi silently added. "If I want to come in early, I will."

"Okay." Ainsley frowned. "That's fair. I just thought—"

"I came in early. Big fucking deal," Gabi snapped before slamming the door shut.

She waited until she heard Ainsley's high heels clicking against the floor indicating she had finally walked away, and then she exited the office and slipped back out the back door. She needed to talk to Pop.

* * *

Gabi had burst into her pop's house with the contract in hand, full of fury and steam over the whole situation. She explained just what he had actually agreed to, and as she'd suspected, he was just as surprised as she was.

"Get out of here," he said, shaking his head in denial. "Nicky told me that—"

She cut him off. "Nicky told you what Gustare Foods told him to tell people. It wasn't the whole story. Pop, you really signed this thing without reading it? Without discussing it with me?" Her voice rose with her frustration. "Without knowing what you were agreeing to?"

He covered his mouth with his palm and his eyes went watery. His complexion paled. He really didn't know.

"I...uh. I didn't..." he stuttered as he sunk down into his recliner.

Gabi's chest felt hollow. The mistake was made and the contract was signed. Beating Pop up about it wasn't going to make things better. "Pop, we'll figure something out."

"Gabi, I'm sorry." He rubbed at his eyes. She'd never seen her father look so defeated and old. "I can't believe I did this. Are you sure the contract says we will sell?"

She nodded. "I've read and reread this thing. It seems pretty solid." She dropped the papers onto the coffee table. Telling him about his mistake was bad enough, he didn't need to see her lose her composure over her feelings too. She swallowed past the painful lump in her throat and sat on the arm of the recliner, leaning her head against Pop's shoulder, searching for something reassuring to say. "Let's not give up quite yet. I'll contact Callie over at Costa and Natali and see if she can give the contract a quick look. We catered their Christmas party last year and I threw in the cannoli and pizzelle on the house. I figured it wouldn't hurt to have a law firm owe us one. May as well cash it in."

* * *

Gabi functioned like a robot all through lunch, cooking and serving meals on autopilot. Her call to Gustare Foods to see if there was any way to nullify the contract had been futile. According to the rep, the deal was done and they weren't in the habit of releasing contracts just because of seller's remorse. Gabi would either have to make an argument that her father wasn't competent when he signed the agreement or that he made a careless mistake. Neither choice would sit well with her father's pride, and she just couldn't bring herself to do that to him after everything else. The only thing left to do was wait to see if her lawyer friend came through for her and found a loophole, but she wasn't particularly hopeful.

She did her best to swallow her frustration and hold it down, but just a little after noon when Ainsley came into the kitchen with a bus tub full of dirty dishes and asked her if she was feeling better, she lost the battle.

"Feeling better?" Gabi growled the question.

"This morning you seemed a little…out of sorts." Ainsley tugged on the collar of her jacket. "I figured you weren't feeling well or something."

Gabi opened her mouth to spit out a glib response, but good sense prevailed. She remembered some of the additional things her father had agreed to by signing the contract. Like the fucking nondisclosure clause. Just like Nicky had advised, it was all in there. And it explicitly stated the staff was not to be informed about the change in management until it officially occurred. Holding a discussion with Ainsley about the specifics of the contract in front of the kitchen staff could very well invoke penalties. The last thing she wanted to do was lose money on top of losing their restaurant. She took the tub from Ainsley and tipped her head toward the dish room to indicate she should follow her. They could have at least a few minutes of privacy in there.

"You're not just here at D'Angelo's to help us transition through Pop's retirement. You're here because Gustare Foods is taking over the restaurant," she whispered loudly enough to be heard over the dishwasher, but not so loudly that her voice would carry out of the room. "I read the contract for myself."

"That's right." Ainsley looked confused. "What's the problem?"

"The problem is, there was a misunderstanding, and when Pop signed the contract he thought Gustare Foods was only coming in to assist with the transition to me taking over for him. He thought this was just a temporary thing."

"Are you seriously telling me your father didn't know the contract he signed was an agreement to sell the restaurant? Did he think Gustare Foods was agreeing to pay him just for the hell of it?"

"I'm telling you he didn't know." Gabi's ears felt impossibly hot with embarrassment. "I sure as hell didn't know."

Ainsley frowned, but not in an angry or annoyed way. It was more…sad. "But didn't he read what he was signing?"

"You've been here long enough to know how Pop is." Gabi slammed her fist on the steel table in frustration. "If it's not a food—not an ingredient—the details don't matter to him. He thought you were coming in here to help us deal with the transition. Like a consultant. I assumed we were paying you rather than the other way around."

"We *are* helping you deal with the transition," Ainsley insisted. "Only when—"

"Only when you're done helping, the restaurant is yours and we're out on the street."

Ainsley crossed her arms. "I wouldn't exactly say *out on the street*. Gustare Foods is paying him a fair price."

"Do not give me more of your company-line crap." The muscles in Gabi's shoulders tensed up and heat crept up her neck. She struggled to keep her voice even. "Do you have any idea how hard it was for me to tell my father he made a mistake that cost him our family business and there's nothing we can do about it?"

"Look, I'm really sorry about the misunderstanding, but he signed the contract. I don't think there's anything we can do about that." Ainsley really did look sorry, but she flicked her gaze across the kitchen toward the swinging doors, obviously still concerned about what was going on in the dining room. Always Gustare Foods' steward. "We still have lunch guests out front, and I need to get back out there. Let's talk more about this after work, okay?"

As they stepped out of the dish room, Gabi surveyed the kitchen. The kitchen she grew up in. Year after year of her father standing at the stove creating delicious dishes, at the service window calling out orders, commanding, and receiving, respect from the D'Angelo's staff no matter what he was doing or how he was doing it. She remembered being a kid building forts out of empty produce boxes in the alley behind the restaurant while her pop opened the restaurant on the weekends, and later, as a tween and teen standing right beside him at the stove learning the secret to making her great-grandmother's marinara—a recipe legendary in Bloomfield. And even after Gabi went off to make her way out in the world, when she failed and was at her lowest and came back home to try to start over afresh, the restaurant and the community welcomed her back with open arms. She owed them everything.

How could this have happened?

Tears burned the corners of her eyes. *Great.* To top off the humiliation of her family accidentally selling the restaurant to Gustare Foods, now she was going to cry about it in front of a Gustare Foods employee? *Absolutely not.*

Ainsley looked back pitifully as she reached to put a hand on her shoulder. "Gabriella, please don't—"

"Get out." She shrugged off Ainsley's touch. Blood was pounding in her ears, and she needed to be alone to pull herself together. Or to scream. Or just be somewhere other than there with Ainsley. Her pulse was racing, her face was hot, and she needed to fucking get away from her. "Get the hell out of my kitchen."

"I'm not the one who—"

"NOW. GET OUT NOW."

Ainsley's eyes widened before she turned and left through the swinging doors back into the dining room where she belonged.

"Fucking FUCK." Gabi grabbed the nearest thing, a soup ladle, and flung it across the kitchen. The clank and clatter as it hit the door of the walk-in cooler startled Brian, who up to that point had been doing his damnedest to ignore her outburst. Throwing something felt somewhat satisfying, but it did nothing to stop her head pounding.

"You need to cool off. Take a walk," Brian suggested, barely looking up from the eggplant he was breading.

"Yeah," Gabi growled and made a beeline for her office, slamming the door behind her. Only then did she let her angry tears fall.

CHAPTER FOURTEEN

Ainsley stayed out of Gabi's way for the rest of her shift, and the moment the dining room had recovered from lunch service, she left the restaurant, relieved to have the evening off and the freedom to stay far away from D'Angelo's.

One hundred percent, she did not deserve the way Gabi had yelled at her in the kitchen. It wasn't Ainsley's fault that Bruno hadn't read what he was signing. And how was she to know? It wasn't even Gustare Foods' fault, really. Maybe Gustare Foods would even show D'Angelo's some grace if Ainsley went to them and explained what had happened—that Bruno didn't know what he was agreeing to and just followed what a buddy had done. Perhaps they could come to some sort of settlement. But after how Gabi treated her that afternoon, Ainsley wasn't exactly in the mood to do her any favors.

The afternoon sun was shining as she walked through Bloomfield back to Ruby's, but she barely noticed the birds chirping, or the delicious offerings in the window display at Rossi's Deli, or even the happy buzz of those frolicking in

Friendship Park. She couldn't think about anything but the anger that had flashed in Gabi's eyes as she ordered her out of the kitchen. Right when they were finally starting to work well together, and finally getting together outside of work as well. How could Gabi treat her like that after all the time they'd spent together and everything they'd shared? It felt like a betrayal and it made her stomach roil.

Although, Gabi's not knowing about the sale did explain why she was always talking so big about being in charge of the restaurant and how she seemed to have absolutely zero plans to let go of the place or even what she was going to do next. Poor thing, she must have been completely blindsided when she realized what was going on. *No. No excuses.* Gabi's disappointment didn't give her a pass for the way she'd acted that afternoon.

Ainsley was still stewing about it as she climbed Ruby's front porch steps and dug through her bag for her keys. Before she could get them into the lock, Ruby appeared through the screen door of her unit.

"Ainsley!" She grinned. "Perfect timing. I've just put on the kettle. Come in and have some tea and cookies with me."

"I don't know, Ruby." She continued to fumble with the lock. "I'm probably not very good company right now. I had a rough day at work."

Ruby tsk-tsked. "Now, I'm sure it's nothing a lady lock can't fix."

The keys slipped from her hands and hit the concrete porch with a jangle. Ainsley bit back the urge to scream in frustration. She wouldn't stoop to behaving like Gabi. She opened her mouth to explain there was no way tea and cookies could make her feel better, not even a flaky, powder-sugar-coated, cream-filled... "You have lady locks?"

"Oh, yes dear. From Luca's—baked fresh this morning." Ruby held open the screen door. "Come on in."

Ainsley followed her into the kitchen where a tray of goodies was waiting as if Ruby knew she would need a little something sweet to balance out her day. While Ruby poured the tea, Ainsley selected one of the lady locks and a pizzelle.

"So, what happened today to put you in this mood?" Ruby asked, joining her at the table. "How could anybody be grumpy while surrounded by all that delicious food at D'Angelo's?"

Ainsley barked a bitter laugh and nearly choked on her cookie. "That's a question for Gabriella D'Angelo herself."

"Did you girls have a disagreement?"

Ainsley recalled the pained expression on Gabi's face as she ordered her out of the kitchen. Disagreement was putting it mildly. It wasn't so much a disagreement, as it was Gabi refusing to face reality and taking it out on her. But she knew better than to reveal details of the contract between D'Angelo's and Gustare Foods. Even to a kind, little old lady who was feeding her sweets to try to cheer her up after a rough day. "Something like that," she conceded.

"But you girls are friends. You'll work it out."

"Not if she keeps yelling so much," Ainsley said around a mouthful of cookie. "It's not my fault she didn't get her way today. It's not my fault she couldn't hack it in New York and had to come home to the family business. Sometimes that's just the way the…well, the cookie crumbles." She grinned at her own cleverness and popped the last bite of pizzelle in her mouth.

Ruby tittered with her tinkly-bell laughter. "She's probably not really yelling. She's just Italian. I don't know what happened between the two of you, but I can almost guarantee the yelling wasn't truly about you." She grabbed Ainsley's hand and gave it a kindly squeeze. "But where did you get the idea that Gabi came back to Bloomfield because she couldn't hack it in New York?"

"She told me all about it." Ainsley shrugged and took a sip of tea and let the heat chase the tension in her jaw away. How did she let that confrontation in the kitchen freak her out so much? She'd faced disgruntled clients before and none of them had gotten under her skin like this. But Gabi was more than just a client. They had a personal relationship too. She couldn't deny it—that was the real reason she was so shaken. "She told me she was a chef at a fancy restaurant in the city and the job didn't work out for her. She ended up coming home and working at her family's restaurant. I think that pretty much paints a picture."

Ruby nodded thoughtfully as she stirred another spoonful of sugar into her tea. "All the things you just said may be true, but there's a difference between *couldn't hack it* and *preferring something else*. Gabi had a fancy job in a fancy restaurant doing something she trained long and hard to do. But it didn't bring her joy. Not like working at D'Angelo's with her family."

Was that what Gabi said? When she told the story, Gabi seemed like she viewed her homecoming as a sign of failure. But the way Ruby told it, Gabi had simply made a choice. She wanted to be in Pittsburgh instead of New York. She made a choice. "I guess I misunderstood. I didn't realize what was at the root of her decision. She didn't explain it that way."

"Oh my. Yes. She did her time at the big, fancy restaurant. She lived the New York City life, but Gabi's heart has always been here with her family and the community. With D'Angelo's. Not because it *has* to be, but because she *wants* it to be." Ruby peered over her teacup, shooting Ainsley a knowing look. "Gabriella D'Angelo is a pretty special woman, but I think you already know that."

Gabi's heart was with D'Angelo's. Wasn't that the truth. It made Ainsley think of the Gabi's gold-heart necklace. Her mother's necklace. Gabi must feel like Gustare Foods is ripping her heart right out of her. No wonder she yelled. She looked at Ainsley and saw the face of the corporation that was taking something so very dear away from her. Gabi had no control over it, and the poor woman had no idea that it was coming. She probably never wanted to see Ainsley again, a thought that made Ainsley's stomach drop. Because Ruby was right—she knew damn well how special Gabi was.

* * *

After Ainsley finished her tea and cookies and Ruby had shooed her away from helping to tidy up in the kitchen, she returned to her side of the duplex. It was still too early to call it a day and crash out on the couch in sweatpants for the evening, but she didn't exactly feel like going out either. Since starting at

D'Angelo's, the only place she'd really gone was…D'Angelo's. Or out with Gabi.

She was restless thinking about her conversation with Ruby, and that hurt look in Gabi's eyes. And did Mr. D'Angelo want to yell at her like that too? Ainsley was pacing her third lap of the living room with that same heartsick feeling that had begun during tea, when it finally struck her that maybe there *was* something she could do about it. She was the liaison between Gustare Foods and D'Angelo's. She could at least make a phone call and see if there was a loophole that would let the D'Angelo family out of their contract. Maybe Linda could help them.

"No, sorry. I can't." Linda didn't really sound sorry. She sounded annoyed. "Mr. D'Angelo made the decision to sign the contract. The deal is done."

"But he didn't understand what he was agreeing to. He thought we were just consultants he was bringing in to help with the transition when he retired. He didn't know he was agreeing to sell the restaurant to Gustare Foods. Surely we have some responsibility to explain the contract to the other party involved."

"We absolutely do not. It is incumbent on the party signing the contract to understand exactly what they are agreeing to." Another annoyed sigh came across the line. "It's regrettable that Bruno is displeased with his decision to sell, but it was his decision. Ainsley, this is not my problem. But it is *your* problem because this is your contract to see through. You're responsible for finalizing this purchase."

Finally, a ray of light. "If the purchase is my responsibility, then can't I decide to call it off? This is all a misunderstanding. It's not fair to make the D'Angelos go through with it if they don't want to sell."

"Not fair?" Linda scoffed. "Is Mr. D'Angelo a competent adult? Is he capable of making decisions? Yes, he is. So the only thing that's unfair here is that he doesn't want to hold up his end of the deal. And now it's your job to keep things at the restaurant going smoothly until Gustare Foods officially takes over. This is your job. You know how to do your job, don't you?"

Oof. This situation was in no way a reflection of Ainsley's ability to do her job properly. She cared about the people she was working with. That was part of what made her so good at what she did for a living. "Of course I do. I just care about the D'Angelos. That's not a bad thing, is it? Come on, Linda, the man made a mistake. There's got to be something we can do for him. What if they decide to challenge this and take us to court?"

"Litigation is not everybody's go-to move," Linda scoffed. Litigation wasn't Ainsley's go-to move either. She'd only threatened it one time in her life. One time, and it had been totally valid. Linda damn well knew that. And that it had been a very different situation. "Besides, we're not new to this business. We've been challenged before, and we've always come out victorious. Our contract is airtight and will one hundred percent hold up in court. But they're not going to take us to court. We're a big corporation. They're small...potatoes. See what I did there? I made a food joke, because that's what these people are. A joke. This deal is going through. See it through, Ainsley."

Linda insulting the D'Angelos didn't make Ainsley feel better about the situation. The only thing it did was remind her how damn cold her boss could be. But she also knew somewhere inside Linda—probably somewhere way down deep—was a tiny little soft spot. Or at least there used to be. Ainsley had witnessed it once or twice. And maybe she could access it again. "Come on, Linda. Please. Won't you reconsider? For me?"

A silence stretched across the line that sent an uneasy, yet somehow quite familiar, chill up her spine. She'd said too much. Pushed too far. Linda was undoubtedly displeased.

"I'll tell you what, Ainsley, here's what I'll do *for you*. If you want to dissolve the contract with the D'Angelos, that's fine, but I want your letter of resignation on my desk in the morning. If we call off the deal, your career with Gustare Foods is over. Is that what you want?"

Ainsley's stomach twisted. Was Linda going to fire her? Her job at Gustare Foods was her whole life. She'd moved from town to town for it, prioritizing work over everything else. She couldn't not have her job. She felt terrible for Mr. D'Angelo and for Gabi—for their whole family losing their restaurant. But she couldn't lose her job.

"No. That's…that's not what I want," Ainsley almost whispered, afraid that if she spoke too loudly she would upset the balance, tip Linda into deciding she was unfit to do her job. "I'll finish the job at D'Angelo's. I'll get it ready for Gustare Foods to come in and take it over."

"Good choice." Linda's shit-eating grin came across the line. "Let me give you a little advice, Ainsley. You're getting too close to these people. Take a step back. Create some distance. Focus on your job, and don't let me down. We're not going to have another conversation like this one."

"No, ma'am. We won't," Ainsley replied, but Linda had already hung up. She didn't care if Ainsley understood or how she felt. She never did. And she clearly didn't care about the D'Angelos. She only cared about the job. Gustare Foods was the only thing that mattered to her, apparently. A sour tang filled her mouth, and she swallowed hard, trying to stave it off as the realization hit her—Linda's assessment sounded mighty familiar. Was she as heartless as Linda when it came to work?

She would do her job—she would keep her word. But she wasn't going to step back. She didn't want distance. She would find some way to make this a little easier for the D'Angelos. She would find some way to help them.

CHAPTER FIFTEEN

Gabi's mood didn't improve much during dinner service that evening. After she'd barked at the kitchen staff a few times, they wised up and avoided her as much as possible, leaving her with plenty of space to simmer like the big pot of sauce on the stove. When things slowed down sometime around eight o'clock, she ventured out to the bar. She could use a drink and there was no risk of running into Ainsley. Her guess was she would stay far away for as long as she could. She cringed inwardly, remembering Ainsley's shocked look before she'd turned and hightailed it out of there.

She slid onto the empty stool next to her father who was sharing a bottle of red with Uncle Sal. Danielle spotted her and pulled her a draft of her favorite IPA. "Hey, Pop. Sal."

Sal stood and drained the last of the wine in his glass. "I better get home before Mary Louise comes looking for me." He clapped a hand on his brother's shoulder and kissed Gabi on the top of the head before leaving.

"Hey, kid," her father said, shifting on his stool to face Gabi. "Hell of a day, huh?"

"You're telling me." Gabi took a big swig of beer. "I really tore into Ainsley about everything. Probably scared the hell out of her. I wouldn't be surprised if she never speaks to me again. That's definitely what I deserve. But I was just so damn mad. Gustare Foods is not going to let us out of the contract, Pop, and I heard back from Callie over at Costa and Natali. She said we can try to take Gustare to court, but they had no obligation to make sure you understood the document, and the contract itself was completely legitimate. It will be a crapshoot if the judge would find in our favor. I don't know if there's anything we can really do to stop the sale."

"You should be mad at me, not her. I was the jagoff who accidentally sold the restaurant." A wry grimace crossed his face. "You were upset, that's understandable. She'll forgive you. Don't worry." He was silent for a beat before adding, "That Ainsley, she's pretty special to you, huh?"

"Yeah." *Oh God, yikes.* The answer was reflexive, not something she intended to say. At all. "No. I mean, she didn't deserve to be the brunt of my anger and I feel bad about it."

"I'm the one you should be yelling at." He had the good grace to ignore her slip of the tongue. "You must be pissed off at me. I did this to us—to you—and I'm so sorry. I acted in haste. I heard Nicky Russo talking about how Gustare Foods eased him into taking over the restaurant and he didn't have to worry about tying up all kinds of loose ends because they were there handling things, and I just didn't pay attention to the details. I didn't ask any questions; I just signed the damned thing without reading it, or discussing it with you, or even our lawyer. I acted in haste. It may be a family trait—or curse—be warned."

"I know a thing or two about acting without thinking," Gabi confessed. Of course, her father was already aware of that. Sometimes it just felt better to admit your flaws out loud, and after lashing out at Ainsley earlier, she was feeling pretty flawed. So much for her promise to move forward with better behavior.

It must have shown on her face because her father put his hand over hers. The warmth of holding her pop's hand was comforting. It still had the same magical calming effect that it did when she was a kid.

"Gabriella, maybe this could be a good thing for you. Maybe it's time to walk away from our little neighborhood restaurant. You don't have to be stuck here with your old man anymore. Don't you want to move on to bigger and better things?"

"Pop, I've tried all that. And I just wanted to come back here. This is what I want. Our perfectly imperfect family restaurant in the neighborhood where I grew up. That's what I learned those years in New York City. I'm happiest right here in Bloomfield, keeping our family recipes alive."

"And I've ruined that for you now. You must be furious with me."

"No, Pop. Never." Gabi took another long drink. She couldn't bear the shine of tears in her father's eyes. "I'm angry with Gustare Foods, but not you. You're the one who gave me those family recipes and traditions I cherish. I'll carry them with me forever. Nobody can take them from me, and that's what really matters. Whether we have the restaurant or not, I have that. And I'll always be grateful for everything you've given me. That's not a building, or pots and pans in a kitchen—it's love. It's family and it's love."

He took another sip of wine and wiped his face with a cocktail napkin. "How the hell did you get to be so smart?"

"I learned from the best." Gabi felt a little lighter after talking it through, but there was still the burn of worry in the pit of her stomach. "But don't give me too much credit. I have no idea what I'm going to do with my life now."

"I have a feeling you'll figure that out."

* * *

On her walk into work the next morning, Gabi picked up donuts from Luca's in an attempt to smooth things over with her kitchen staff, and while shoving two zeppole in his face seemed to make things right with Brian, she was still nervous about facing Ainsley.

What if Ainsley decided she didn't want to deal with Gabi, and someone else from Gustare Foods showed up to take over her job? Ainsley had started out as a real pain in the ass—well, their first night together excepted—but in the past few weeks she'd really grown on her. Would she go as far as to say Ainsley was special to her? They'd both agreed anything between them was purely temporary—just while Ainsley was in town. And she had to admit, they'd been getting on famously up to that point. But, special?

Still, riding out the rest of her time at D'Angelo's with Ainsley until the official handover was going to be hard enough without dealing with additional Gustare Foods personnel showing up and rubbing it in that D'Angelo's as she knew it was no more. She was going to have to make peace with working alongside Ainsley despite her association with an evil corporation which basically tricked her father out of the family business. At least she had a minute to breathe and think through how she might do that.

It wasn't too long into the morning prep routine when Ainsley came through the swinging doors into the kitchen. For a moment they just stared at each other. Then they said at the same time, "We need to talk."

They both laughed. Gabi's was rooted in relief that Ainsley was at least still willing to speak to her. "But I am going to put you to work while we do," Gabi said as she handed Ainsley a peeler and nodded at the ten-pound bag of potatoes on the steel prep table. "We've still got a restaurant to open for lunch."

"Fair," Ainsley agreed. "So, I—"

"No. Me first," Gabi insisted. She was the one who had behaved badly. Ainsley had done nothing wrong. Gabi needed to make things right between them. "I'm sorry that I yelled at you yesterday. I was angry about the Gustare Foods contract, and I took it out on you. And that was unfair. That was wrong and I'm sorry."

Ainsley nodded pensively and studied the potato in her hand. When she raised her gaze again her expression was soft with forgiveness. "Thank you for saying that. I know you had just received upsetting news, and honestly, I'm so sorry about how it all played out. I wish things were different, but I put in a call to my boss at Gustare Foods and she said there's nothing you can do. Bruno signed the contract and the deal is set. He could try to take Gustare Foods to court to dispute it, but…"

"But Gustare Foods has their big corporate lawyers and Pop probably doesn't stand a chance because the contract is pretty solid. Yeah, I had an attorney look it over." Gabi blew out a long sigh. "What if our loyal customers stage a boycott? Maybe some protests and bad press would scare off Gustare Foods, get them to reconsider."

Ainsley shook her head. "You can't tell the customers about the change in management, or you'll be in breach of the nondisclosure agreement. Besides, even if there is a public-relations blip or some kind of boycott, Gustare Foods will just shut down their version of D'Angelo's and retool the restaurant. It's happened before. The community response eventually fizzles out and the company just reopens the place under another name."

There it was, confirmed—they were powerless in this situation. "What the hell am I going to do now?"

"Well, I have been thinking about that." Ainsley smiled and straightened her posture. Snapping back into Business Management Barbie mode. Only this time Gabi noticed how sexy that look was on her. "According to the contract, Gustare Foods gets the restaurant—the physical location and the D'Angelo's name. But the recipes—your sauces and Nonna's secret spice mix—Gustare Foods doesn't care about them. They weren't included in the contract because they don't plan to use them. Once they take over, they'll use their own suppliers and their Italian restaurant operations-and-procedures manual moving forward. You know how they love their checklists."

"I do," Gabi said and tossed another peeled potato into the plastic tote filled with water. Only a few weeks ago those checklists were the bane of her existence and now they felt like a saving grace. The family still owned their recipes. She paused her food prep and let relief settle in. "I can't believe they aren't going to use the recipes. That's the whole essence of D'Angelo's. That's the best part—what makes us special."

"Gabi, focus. This is not a slight toward your family in this case—it's a good thing." Ainsley grabbed another potato—such a good multitasker. "You can take your family recipes and open up a new restaurant. You just can't call it 'D'Angelo's.' But you can use some variation on the name."

"Oh my God." An excited hum stirred in Gabi's chest. "I can open a new restaurant. I'll still have the same menu—all the great D'Angelo's recipes. I'll call it Gabriella's, or Bruno's, or Nonna D's. Okay, I'll workshop that. But I can open a new restaurant. Oh! There's an empty storefront just a couple of blocks over. It would be a great location for a new place."

"Well, no." Ainsley shook her head. "Not in the neighborhood. The contract stipulates you won't open a new restaurant in Bloomfield for the next seven years. But you can do it somewhere else."

"Not here in Bloomfield though. I don't know. I can't imagine having a place somewhere else."

"Okay. I understand. There are other things you could do." Ainsley didn't seem ready to give up, rather, she looked like she was just revving up. "Like a food truck. You couldn't park it within the radius stipulated in the contract but think about it this way—you'd be taking a taste of Bloomfield out into the world. Or at least the greater Pittsburgh area."

"I like the sound of that," Gabi mused. It still honored her roots. She'd still be cooking the family's beloved recipes. "I'd have a lot to learn about the food truck business. It's a good idea though, and I'll think about it. Thanks."

"I'm not done yet." Ainsley's eyes were bright. She was a fighter, that was for sure. "Like you said, your family recipes are the essence of D'Angelo's. Your spice mix and your sauces are incredible. They keep people coming back for more. What if you sold them in markets? Grocery stores. It would be a whole new business opportunity. I know it's not the same as having your restaurant, but maybe it will be a small consolation. It could carry you over until you figure out your next step—the food truck or the restaurant somewhere else, or whatever you decide. You could debut the products at the Slice of Italy Festival. Really kick things off right."

This time when their gazes met over the peeled potatoes, Gabi felt a pleasurable tingling in her neck and cheeks. "You've really thought this through."

"I have." Ainsley set down her peeler. "Bloomfield has really grown on me. I like D'Angelo's and your family. And I like..." She glanced at the swinging doors that led to the dining room—her domain—and shook her head. "Anyway, I want to help. Gustare Foods is my employer, so I have to complete my assignment. It's my job. But between you and me, I think this whole situation is unfair. I want to help you however I can. If you'll let me, I mean."

For the first time since Gabi had laid eyes on that Gustare Foods contract she felt a spark of hope. The situation sucked, and she was going to lose D'Angelo's. But she wasn't alone, and she would figure out what to do next. "I'd actually love that."

CHAPTER SIXTEEN

Ainsley hustled around the dining room with last-minute preparations for her first official meeting with the Slice of Italy Committee. She figured helping with the festival would be one little thing she could do for Gabi and for the neighborhood while she was still in Bloomfield. This time around she was the one pushing tables together to prepare for the group's arrival. Of course, this time the group booking was on the dining room schedule per Gustare Foods' rules.

"Can we get a large charcuterie board out here, please?" she called into the kitchen through the service window. While she waited, she filled pitchers with soft drinks and grabbed glasses for the expected crowd.

"The large board, huh?" Gabi's voice held a teasing note as she delivered it to the table. "You're going all out for this meeting."

"It's my first one. I want to make a good impression."

"So, you're bribing them with cured meats and olives." Gabi laughed.

Since Gabi had accepted Ainsley's offer of help, there had been a definite shift in their relationship. It was as if they'd come to an understanding—they were on the same team as opposed to combatants. And that was a big part of why Ainsley was so nervous about this meeting going well. She wanted to show Gabi that she was committed to the festival and that she could fit in with the folks from the community. And that she would be there for Gabi no matter what happened.

As the committee members trickled in, Ainsley and Gabi worked as a double act—Ainsley pouring drinks, Gabi greeting each person and making introductions.

Ainsley made a deliberate effort to learn the name of each person. There were David and Jon from Luca's Bakery, Jennifer the librarian from the community center, Lisa who with her husband owned the hardware store down the block, a thirty-something named Jack, and Hailey, or as Ainsley still thought of her, Little Red. But as the meeting got down to business, she found it was a struggle to tear her eyes away from Gabi.

Ainsley had become accustomed to Gabi calling the shots in the kitchen, the bold, bigger-than-life personality running the show. In this situation, she was patient and reserved. Quiet, but thoughtful. Sitting backlit by the beams of sunshine coming through the big front window of the restaurant, she was absolutely stunning.

"I'm pleased to share that we have an additional five thousand dollars in sponsorship since we last met two weeks ago," Gabi reported when it was her turn to speak. "And I'm hopeful we'll have double that by the next time we meet."

"That's great news," Lisa said, nodding and making a note on the yellow legal pad in front of her. She tapped her pen against the electric-blue frames of her glasses. "Have you approached Health Spot yet? They used to be such a huge supporter back in the day."

"I have them on my list." Gabi took a thin slice of salami from the charcuterie board. Ainsley's gaze remained fixed on her lips as she chewed. "I'm just trying to make sure I have the right contact. I want to get to the right person for maximum impact—maybe someone who knows about Slice of Italy, who's been involved with the festival in the past. I thought maybe I could ask someone who was on the committee before the great shutdown."

Ainsley was still staring at Gabi's mouth. Mesmerized. *Snap out of it!* She needed to pay attention and act like part of the group. Health Spot, the health enterprise of several hospitals in the Pittsburgh area, could be a great source of monetary support for the festival if the committee could convince them to get on board. And if she could assist Gabi with this task it would really show how useful she could be to the committee. "I can help you get to the bottom of that."

The smile Gabi flashed in her direction brightened the room.

"That settles that," David concluded. "Hailey, give us an update on the entertainment. Any new groups added to the entertainment lineup?"

Ainsley made a renewed effort to stay focused on the conversation for the rest of the meeting. Little Red gave the latest details on the dance troupe set to perform. Jack showed the mockup of the graphic he designed for the flyers, advertisements, and T-shirts they could sell at the festival. The business portion of the gathering drew to a close and turned to local chitchat. Jennifer's son had taken a field trip with his fifth-grade history class earlier that week, and Ainsley caught a word that seemed out of context.

"Wait, an *incline*?" she inquired.

"They rode the Duquesne Incline up to Mt. Washington," Jennifer clarified.

"The...what?" Ainsley tried again.

Jon turned to Gabi. "You haven't taken your lady friend on the Incline?"

"She's not my lady friend," Gabi and Ainsley both replied simultaneously.

"I'm sorry, I just assumed..." Jon laughed. "The way the two of you have been making eyes at each other while we've been sitting here, it just seemed like you were—well, never mind."

"Making eyes? I don't know about that," Gabi mumbled, but her cheeks flushed a telltale rosy hue.

Was it possible that Gabi had feelings that were more than temporary for her too?

"Lady friend or not, you need to remedy that," Lisa chimed in. "You can't let someone new to our fair city miss out on the marvel that is the Duquesne Incline. Make a date to take her."

"Yes." Ainsley joined the pile, unable to resist teasing her. "Take me on a date to the Incline."

Gabi's cheeks went another shade brighter, but she relented. "Okay, fine. It's a date. Tonight, we ride."

CHAPTER SEVENTEEN

Gabi stared at her image in the full-length mirror in her bedroom. She was on her third outfit, but she'd finally landed on cream-colored jeans and an indigo light-knit top. Her simple gold chain with a tiny heart charm topped it off—the only personal belonging of her mother's she possessed. She paused, pressed a finger against the charm and said a silent prayer that the night would go well. She was taking a risk treating this night out as a real date when they'd both agreed this thing between them was only temporary. She didn't want Ainsley to feel like she was overstepping any boundaries.

She slipped on her suede ankle boots. What was she feeling so nervous about anyway? She'd spent plenty of time with Ainsley over the past month. Hell, she'd seen the woman naked on that first night. Her cheeks went warm all over again remembering the long, graceful lines of Ainsley's beautiful body and how the two of them had spent hours tangled up in her sheets. She'd worked so hard to push those thoughts out of her head and keep things professional and now recalled that anything between them was only temporary. But lately with all the crap Gustare Foods had put them through, she'd started to feel like all bets were off. Considering the truth of the situation, she and Ainsley weren't really coworkers. Gabi had no intention of staying on staff and working for Gustare Foods once they officially took over, even if they wanted her to, and she wasn't sure where Ainsley would end up when her assignment in Bloomfield was complete. Regardless, in a couple of months they wouldn't even be work-adjacent.

On the way out, she grabbed the bouquet she'd picked up earlier. Ainsley had said she wanted a date, and that was what she was going to get. If they were going to do this, Gabi was determined to do it properly. As she walked the four blocks to Ainsley's place, her chest felt like it was full of helium. When she spotted Ainsley standing on the front stoop, smiling in the soft light of the setting sun and waving at her, Gabi really thought she might just float away. Happiness—it was a powerful thing.

"Hey there," Ainsley called out her greeting. She was remarkably nimble as she bounced down the cement steps in her strappy espadrilles. "I hope I'm dressed appropriately for inclining."

Gabi laughed and handed Ainsley the flowers. "We're not going to *incline*, we're going to *ride* the Incline. But you are dressed perfectly for it. You look gorgeous."

Ainsley's purple-hued floral midi dress layered with a white pleather jacket really made her bright blue eyes pop. The kind of eyes into which one could stare forever. "Thank you." She gave Gabi's hand a squeeze but continued to hold on while they stood there on the sidewalk grinning at each other.

Gabi's gaze only drifted from Ainsley's eye to focus on her plump, pink-glossed lips. For some reason, tonight they especially looked like an absolute dream to kiss.

"Oh my, that's a gorgeous bouquet." Ruby's voice interrupted the moment. Had she been watching them from her porch that whole time? "Give them here and I'll put them in some water so you girls can get going."

Ten minutes later their rideshare dropped them off at the Duquesne Incline station.

"Are you excited?" Gabi asked Ainsley as she paid the attendant.

"I'm a little nervous," Ainsley confessed. "I don't know what I was expecting, but it wasn't this."

Gabi followed Ainsley's apprehensive gaze to the side of Mt. Washington and the steel tracks heading straight up the side. The Incline—looking like a mini trolley car—was slowly descending the slope toward the station.

"Don't worry. If you get scared you can always hold my hand."

Moments later, they were seated side by side on a wooden bench inside the cabin, waiting for other passengers to board. First was a family of four. The two young children immediately pressed their faces to the window, curious to see all they could. Gabi recalled doing the same when she was their age. Then another couple entered the car and cuddled together on one of the benches. There was room for about eighteen people if the car was full, but fortunately it seemed this would not be a packed trip. Finally, the door was closed and as the car jerked to begin its ascent, Ainsley grabbed her hand.

"Seriously, you're not afraid of heights, are you?" Gabi asked, inwardly holding her breath. The whole plan for the night would be a bust if her answer was yes.

"No. I'm just happy to be here with you." Ainsley rested her head against Gabi's shoulder.

Gabi signed contentedly and watched as Pittsburgh dropped away below them. She inhaled the musk of old wood and grease, the scent of Pittsburgh history. "This is one of two Inclines we have in the city. The other is the Monongahela Incline. They were originally constructed to carry cargo up and down Mt. Washington, but eventually they were used for passengers as well. There used to be more than just the two, but as more people started driving cars instead of walking, most of them closed, until there were only these two left. They were restored in the '60s and have been Pittsburgh icons ever since."

The ride only lasted a few minutes, but Gabi knew the best part was at the top. She led Ainsley to the observation deck and spread her arms wide. "Behold the Golden Triangle in all its glory."

Ainsley gasped. "Oh my God, this view is amazing." She walked all the way to the rail to take it all in. "But what did you call it?"

"The Golden Triangle," Gabi repeated. "Look how the rivers come together." She pointed at the city below as she spoke. "The Allegheny and the Monongahela come together to make the Ohio River. And the space between the rivers form—"

"A triangle," Ainsley finished. "Oh! And the fountain."

"That's right—Point State Park, where we had our picnic. The Fort Pitt Museum is there too, remember?" Gabi nodded. "Jon was right—I really do have a lot of Pittsburgh to show you. By the way, I'm sorry the committee put you on the spot about this date."

"I'm not." Ainsley continued to look at the city as she slipped her hand into Gabi's again. "I've been waiting for this for a while."

"Going on a date with me, or seeing Pittsburgh?"

"Both, if I'm being honest." Ainsley was smiling when she turned to face her. "I've wanted to go on a date with you. It's just with working together, and my temporary status in town, and trying to keep things professional between us after, well, you know." She bit her bottom lip.

Gabi didn't need the visual to remind her about that night they'd spent together before work got in the way, but excitement stirred in her core anyway. "Oh, I know."

"But with everything lately, in the past week or so, I just thought…" She shrugged.

"You thought, 'screw Gustare Foods,' right?" Gabi filled in the blanks.

"Well, Gustare Foods *is* still my employer, so I might say it more gently, but basically something like that."

That light, floaty feeling was back in Gabi's chest. If there had been any doubt before, it had gone now. Not only was this a true date, but Ainsley had just said that she'd been thinking about going out with her for a while. "Then I guess it's a good thing I made dinner reservations. You hungry?"

* * *

Seated at a table with a fantastic view of the city below, they shared a meal and easy conversation, and the more Gabi learned about Ainsley, the more she wanted to know. The minutes just seemed to slip by while they traded stories, but Gabi made sure to keep an eye on the time. She had one more surprise planned for the night. A quick glance at her watch indicated they were still on track.

"Did you like where you were at your last Gustare Foods assignment?" Gabi asked.

"Buffalo? It was fine, but I didn't really see much of it. I spent so much time working, I didn't venture out much. I didn't have anyone to show me around like you've done." Ainsley seemed to reflect on that for a beat. "Even when you thought I was nothing more than Business Management Barbie, you took me to the Strip District. You still showed me around Pittsburgh. Why was that?"

"You'll find us Pittsburghers have a lot of pride in our city. I like to show it off. And, despite our differences, maybe subconsciously I wanted to spend more time with you." Again, Gabi felt her cheeks heat. To offset that confession, she winked and added, "Somewhere you wouldn't feel obligated to tell me what to do."

Ainsley laughed and took the last bite of caffe latte turtle cake they were sharing for dessert. "I've enjoyed this meal so much, and I've had such a lovely evening with you, I'm going to pretend you didn't say that last bit."

"I'm glad to hear you're having a lovely evening, but it's not done yet."

Gabi settled the check and led Ainsley back outside to the observation deck.

"I admit the view of Pittsburgh all lit up at night is breathtaking, but you know we were just here before dinner," Ainsley teased.

Gabi stuck her tongue out in response, but then she pulled Ainsley close, wrapped her arms around her and whispered, "For once, could you just trust that I know what I'm doing?"

Ainsley's lips parted as if she was going to trade quips, but when their eyes locked and her pupils went wide, instead of making a joke she replied, "Gabi D'Angelo, I believe you know exactly what you're doing. And I'm completely enthralled with every single minute of it."

"Good. Because I really like sharing those minutes with you."

As if on cue the sky lit up with colorful fireworks from across the river. It drew gasps from both of them as they took in the spectacle, but only for a moment before Ainsley grabbed onto Gabi again, demanding her attention.

"How did you make this happen?"

"Fireworks night at the ballpark. Another Pittsburgh tradition," Gabi answered as the booming display reverberated in her chest. Her boldness grew with every crash. "And I'm going to kiss you now."

Finally their lips met in the most wonderful, soft and magical kiss made all the sweeter by the flashes of color and light cascading down in the sky above them. When they finally came up for air, Ainsley smiled with puffy lips and lusty eyes. "A girl could get very used to these traditions."

Gabi couldn't agree more.

CHAPTER EIGHTEEN

As the lunch rush ended, Ainsley found herself with one eye on the door as she ran down her front-of-house checklist. She'd restocked the tea bags in the server station and just put on a fresh pot of decaf when she realized it—she was looking forward to seeing the card-club gang. She was pushing their tables together when the first of them arrived.

"Vic, I'll grab your soda." She gestured in an effort to direct the couple to take a seat. "Ida, there's a fresh pot of decaf brewing now."

"Best make a pot of regular for Ruby," Ida reminded her. "Or you'll get an earful."

"I will," Ainsley called back from the station. "But she's always the last one here, so I wanted to get yours going first."

"You're catching on." Vic patted Ainsley's shoulder as she delivered the beverages. "Good girl."

Ainsley's cheeks tingled with pride as she rushed back to the kitchen to check on the group's appetizers. She needn't have worried—as usual, Gabi was ready for her Monday afternoon guests.

"Run the artichoke dip out," Gabi ordered. "I'll plate up my cookies."

"Cookies?" Ainsley quirked an eyebrow at her. "Do we have cookies on the menu?"

She shrugged. "Thought I'd make a treat for my friends."

Ainsley smiled over her shoulder as she pushed through the swinging doors to the dining room, dip and chips in hand.

The rest of the group—George, Gerri, Barb, and even Ruby—had all arrived. Vic was shuffling the deck in preparation for the game. He greeted her—and the food—with a wide smile. "Artichoke dip and chips. My favorite. You know what it reminds me of?" he asked the table at large.

"Here we go again," George groused from the other side of the table. "It's been gone for years, Vic. Get over it."

"Hush, George," Ruby scolded as she reached for her cards. "Let him reminisce."

Ainsley's curiosity piqued, she pulled up a chair and settled in. "What does artichoke dip remind you of?"

"The D'Angelo's lunch buffet." Vic beamed. "Back in the eighties, D'Angelo's held the best lunch buffet for miles. Bruno Senior always put the dip out. There would be chips and bread for dipping, but there was fried ravioli too. Delicious."

"A lunch buffet?" To Ainsley it sounded like a nightmare and definitely a prepandemic concept. "Every day?"

"No," Ida piped up. "Every Friday though. Vic and I would come here on our lunch hour. It was a real treat."

"I remember." Gerri nodded. Her white bob cut shimmied in excitement at recounting the good ol' days. "It really was a treat. We would meet here for lunch—whoever was available— fill up on good food and set our plans for the weekend. Senior would put out a couple of different pizzas, a pasta dish, either chicken or eggplant parm."

"Soup and salad too. It was a feast," Vic concluded as he pointed at Ainsley. "You think you could convince Gabi to bring back the lunch buffet?"

"I'm not sure." Ainsley meant to sound diplomatic. It wasn't Gabi who would object. A buffet actually sounded right up her alley. But the concept would never fly with Gustare

Foods. Maybe she could find a compromise. "What else do you remember about D'Angelo's from back in the day? Any favorite dishes you wish were still on the menu that have disappeared over the years?"

"I don't know about particular dishes." Barb mulled it over while she dumped two packets of sweetener into her coffee. "Bruno kept all the classics on the menu when he took over from Senior. There were some additions when Gabi came back though."

"Oh, like the chicken cordon bleu!" Ruby swayed and rolled her eyes to express the joy the dish brought her.

"You can't mess with the classics." George slapped a hand on the table to emphasize his point. "People expect certain things when they go to an Italian restaurant, and they like what they like. I'll tell you what I miss—the early-bird special." The others nodded and murmured their agreement. It was apparently a sentiment shared by the entire group.

"The early-bird special," Ainsley repeated, somewhat familiar with the concept. "Was it just a discount for coming in early for dinner?"

"A real bargain, I'll tell ya," Vic said. "So what if you eat a couple of hours earlier? Who cares? It was worth it."

Ainsley knew some restaurants had similar deals. She wasn't certain about Gustare Foods' stance on that sort of thing, but if it was popular with the locals, it could be worth exploring. "They simply took a percentage off your bill at the end of the meal?"

"It wasn't like that. There were only certain meals that were on special," Vic explained, between gulps of Diet Coke. "And the meals would change from week to week. I think Bruno just served up whatever he had left over after the weekend. Early-bird special day was always on Monday. Anyway, it was a great deal."

Bruno would take whatever didn't sell over the weekend and unload it by presenting it as the early-bird special. Prevented food waste, brought people in on a day that was traditionally a lower volume day—it was actually pretty brilliant.

Ruby cleared her throat loudly. "I love a cheap meal as much as the next person, but are we going to play cards or just flap our gums all day?"

Ainsley stood and put her hands in the air, surrendering. "Sorry everyone. Get your game on. I'll get back to work." She put a hand on Vic's shoulder. "Thanks for sharing your stories with me."

She returned to the server station but couldn't help peeking at the group as they played cards and snacked and laughed. A group of friends who had shared good times in that dining room for forty years. It was rather amazing when you thought about it. D'Angelo's really had made an impact on the community. It gave her a real sense of pride to be a part of that. And an enormous sense of loss to think that could all be under threat...

* * *

A few hours later as the card club was finishing up their dinner, Ainsley was still sitting at a two-top in the dining room doing some research for the Slice of Italy Festival. Pouring over scans of old committee notes to locate the correct person for Gabi to contact at Health Spot had consumed her for the past hour. She was so deeply engrossed, she didn't hear Ruby approach her table.

"You've been awfully quiet all afternoon," Ruby said, leaning on the back of the chair opposite Ainsley. "I hope it's not because I chased you away from our card game."

"Oh no, Ruby." Ainsley sank back in her seat and stretched her arms over her head. She'd been sitting on that wooden chair too long. Taking a break and moving around a bit would do her some good. "Can I bring you folks anything?"

"Us? We don't need a thing." She shook her head. "I was just worried about you. Staring at that screen all day can't be good for you."

"I agree. But I told Gabi I'd help her, so I can't give up just yet." Ainsley sighed and rubbed her eyes. "Maybe I'm going about this wrong. It would probably be easier if I could just speak to someone who was on the committee back in the festival's heyday. It would be helpful if I could just ask the right person a few questions."

"You've been talking to that someone all day, dear."

She'd been talking to a former committee member in the dining room? Her gaze pulled to the card club. "One of the gang? Are you serious?"

Ruby nodded. "Vic. I'm sure he'd be happy to help."

Ainsley accompanied Ruby back to the table and once again pulled a chair up right next to the former committee member. "Vic, why didn't you tell me you were on the Slice of Italy Committee?"

"You never asked," he replied simply and drained the last of his Diet Coke.

"Fair," Ainsley acknowledged before presenting her deal. "If I promise to work on bringing back D'Angelo's early-bird special, will you answer some questions about the festival's history?"

He covered her folded, pleading hands with his own, weathered and covered in age spots. "How about I just answer your questions because you ask me? And because I like you, kid."

No one ever called Ainsley *kid*. Her father was much too formal. Daughter was a strong term of endearment to him. It had sufficed. But Vic's comforting touch, combined with the warmth in how he called her *kid*, somehow reassuringly bolstered her. Vic was willing to help her. She would help Gabi. Gabi would help the committee and in turn they were helping the neighborhood. The realization clicked into place like the last piece of a puzzle making the total image clear. Together they would make it all work out.

"Let me refill your soda," Ainsley said with a grateful smile, "and then we'll get to the questions."

CHAPTER NINETEEN

Gabi unpacked the mason jars she'd ordered, placing each one neatly in a row on the stainless-steel worktable in front of her. They'd been delivered right before dinner and she had to put them aside, but now that the rush was over, she was ready for a little experimentation with the canning kit she'd borrowed from her nonna.

Ainsley pushed through the swinging doors. "I thought you'd be wrapping up back here," she said, eying the collection of jars. "Instead, it looks like you're fixing to start a project."

"I am." Gabi laughed at Ainsley's bewildered expression. "I've got Nonna's canner and tools, and thought I'd try putting down some sauce tonight."

"You're going to go for it." Ainsley beamed. "I'm proud of you."

"I said I'm going to *try*," Gabi corrected her. No need to get overly excited about a new potential business venture until she dipped her toes in the water. "We'll see how this first batch goes. If it works, maybe I'll do more. Maybe I will sell them at the Slice of Italy Festival like you suggested. Get the product out there, generate some buzz—isn't that what you business-management folks say?"

Ainsley nodded and reached for a clean apron. "You're absolutely correct." She tied the strings and joined Gabi at the worktable. "This isn't what I expected to do with my night, but if you'll have me, I'd love to help."

"I will definitely take you up on that offer."

The women got to work setting up the canner and sterilizing the jars. As they worked, Ainsley told Gabi about her chat with Vic. "He gave me the name of the contact at Health Spot who worked with the committee in the past. I'll call tomorrow morning and set up an appointment for us to meet with him." Ainsley's eyes went wide. "I mean, if you're okay with me coming along."

First Ainsley had asked if Gabi would let her help with the sauce, and now she was asking if it was okay to come along on a committee errand. What was going on here?

"Why do you keep asking if I want to do things with you? I thought I made it pretty clear when I kissed you under the fireworks that I want to do things with you." Wasn't that an understatement? Her gaze locked on Ainsley's plump lips—that mouth she'd kissed while the sky flashed around them. Sure, she'd planned it, but the moment had felt magical somehow anyway. "I want to *lots* of things with you."

"I want to do things with you too," Ainsley said and her tongue darted out to moisten her lips as if she was remembering the kiss too. Gabi could swear she saw a flash of the fireworks reflected in her eyes. "I know I came into D'Angelo's and took charge of things. I was bossy and insistent, and wanted everyone to follow the rules. Gustare Foods' rules. Because that's my job. It's a job I like, and one that I'm really good at. But the Slice of Italy Festival, and this…" She gestured at the canning supplies around them. "These things are yours. I'm here and happy to support you any way I can, but you're calling the shots. I'm just along for the ride. Because I believe in you."

A wild fluttering filled Gabi's chest. Whatever she decided to do next post-D'Angelo's, Ainsley believed in her. And now that she'd heard the words out loud, she realized that whatever her next career move, it was going to be okay because she believed in herself. She'd changed courses before—after New York—and came out better for it. She could do it again.

She wrapped Ainsley in her arms until their hips bumped. Bringing their faces so close she could practically taste the strawberry gloss on Ainsley's lips. "I'm very grateful to have you along for the ride. I think we make a hell of a team."

Finally, their mouths crashed together in a passionate kiss that only deepened as their tongues touched and tangled. All Gabi's worry faded away as she melted into the moment. Until the dishwasher beeped to indicate the sanitizing cycle was over. They both laughed, their mouths still sliding against each other.

"Guess it's time to get back to that teamwork." Ainsley's voice was soft, holding a hint that her resolve could crumble if challenged.

"We're only pressing pause to take care of business," Gabi promised. "This is to be continued."

She was certain of that.

* * *

When the last jar was finally sealed and there was nothing left to do but let them rest, Gabi pulled off her apron, more than ready to call it a day. "We need to let them sit out for twelve hours," she said, tossing her apron into the dirty-linen bin. "My vote is we go home and forget about sauce until tomorrow morning."

"We've been canning it for three hours. I'm pretty sure I'm going to dream about sauce tonight," Ainsley joked.

"It would've taken me a lot longer to do it alone. Thank you for staying to help."

"I didn't mind at all." Ainsley's smile was tired. "It was fun. Plus, I learned a little something about canning."

"I think Nonna is going to be very proud of us." Gabi grabbed her belongings as they headed to the door. The buzzing LED parking lot lights above them punctuated the dark night as she locked up. "Come on, I'll walk you home since I kept you late."

"Are you going to have her taste test the sauce?" Ainsley asked, hitching her purse up on her shoulder as they started down the sidewalk.

Gabi nodded. There was no way she was moving forward without Nonna's blessing. "She has got to give this project her stamp of approval, or I can't go through with it. It wouldn't feel right."

"That's understandable. But I'm sure she's going to be pleased."

"I hope you're right." Gabi felt a flutter in her belly. Ainsley seemed to understand how important Nonna's approval was to her. Bolstered by the good feeling of concord, she grabbed Ainsley's hand.

The two walked silently for a moment, swinging their arms between them. The stars shining above seemed to glow especially brightly—as if to guide their way home. When they finally reached Ainsley's, they paused on the sidewalk in front of the quiet house.

Ainsley turned to her and bit her bottom lip as if considering something. "I know it's been a long day, but do you want to come in and have a cup of tea or something?"

"Tea would be perfection."

Fifteen minutes later, Gabi was sitting on a flower-print couch straight out of the nineties, with a cup of decaf tea she didn't care about and felt much too tired to drink anyway. But she was flooded with a sense of contentedness with Ainsley's head resting on her shoulder in the flickering light of the television. A rerun episode of *Celebrity Cook-Off* filled the screen.

"You probably don't want to watch a show about cooking after working in a kitchen all day." Ainsley's voice was sleepy. It reminded Gabi of that first morning they had woken up together. "Do you want to change the channel?"

"Are you kidding me?" Gabi asked through a yawn. "I love this show."

Before she knew it, her heavy eyelids were closing while she sat right there on the couch, fingers intertwined with Ainsley's, heart happier than she could remember it being in a very long time.

* * *

Gabi awoke the next morning spooning Ainsley on the couch, having shifted at some point in the night. She blinked against the rays of morning sun pouring through the front window. It had been so dark the night before, she hadn't realized how big—and curtain free—the window was. She hadn't meant to stay there all night, but she felt so warm and good pressed up against Ainsley that she certainly wasn't upset about it. She ran her hand up Ainsley's arm and nuzzled her neck.

"Mmm." Ainsley stirred. "Good morning. Oh wait. We slept together here on the couch?"

"It sure seems that way." Gabi kissed her way along her jawbone. God, this was the very best way to start the day. Too bad they'd both been much too tired last night to do anything more than sleeping.

Ainsley seemed to share that sentiment as she twisted to face Gabi and kissed her firmly on the mouth. When she tangled her hands in Gabi's hair and deepened the kiss, Gabi's nipples went insta-hard. It was terribly unfortunate that they couldn't do this all day because they had to—

"Ugh. Crap."

Ainsley pulled back. "That is not a reaction I usually get when doing this."

"I didn't mean the kiss." Gabi laughed and gave her another quick peck on the mouth to emphasize her words. "I meant, what time is it? I've got to get showered up and get my ass back to the restaurant before Brian freaks out about the jars of sauce everywhere while he's trying to complete the morning prep work."

"Ugh. Crap," Ainsley echoed before nibbling on Gabi's earlobe. "Are you sure you have to go?"

Gabi squinted to read the clock on the wall. Already after seven o'clock. Even if she ran home and skipped shaving her legs she would be lucky if she made it back to D'Angelo's by eight. Brian was definitely going to be pissed. "Yeah. We're going to have to call this *to be continued* yet again."

Ainsley growled but rolled onto her back, giving Gabi the space to maneuver her way off the couch. Within five minutes Gabi was out the door, but she didn't even make it off the porch before she was stopped.

"Gabriella, what a pleasant surprise." Ruby, still in a tattered pink housecoat and slippers grinned at her like the cat who ate the canary. "Fancy meeting you on my front porch at seven a.m."

"Good morning, Ruby. I was just, uh..." Why did she feel like she'd been totally busted? She was a grown woman. She could spend the night with someone if she wanted to. She didn't have to explain herself to a nebby neighbor, even if she was Ainsley's landlord. Who happened to look extremely tickled by this turn of events. "I was just hanging out with Ainsley, and now I'm late for work, so I've got to run. Nice to see you though. Have a good day." Before she could babble any more, she ducked her head and descended the steps to the sidewalk.

"It was *very* nice to see you," Ruby called after her, her tinkling-bell laughter accompanying her words. "Especially you with Ainsley."

Gabi couldn't deny it—it was pretty damned nice to be seen with Ainsley as well. With a spring in her step, she hustled home.

CHAPTER TWENTY

Friday morning, Ainsley arrived at Gabi's house dressed in a black pencil skirt and an ivory blouse, a simple but classic strand of pearls around her neck—all business for their Health Spot meeting. Gabi was waiting for her, looking pretty sharp herself in gray dress slacks and a black blazer over an emerald-green cami that perfectly complemented the deep-brown hue of her eyes. Stunning.

"I thought we'd just take my car," Gabi said by way of a greeting. "I figure it's cheaper to drive in ourselves and park than hire a ride."

Ainsley was sure she'd misheard. "Wait, you have a car?"

"Yep," Gabi said as she led her around the house to the street that ran behind it where a navy-blue Mazda sedan was parked. "I bought it used when I moved back to Pittsburgh. I don't drive a ton, but it's nice to have the option." Gabi opened the passenger-side door for her which Ainsley found charming, and they were on their way.

During the drive through the city, Gabi answered Ainsley's questions about the neighborhoods surrounding the downtown area and about Pittsburgh itself. She was especially surprised to learn that Pittsburgh has more bridges than any city in the world.

"That can't be true," Ainsley insisted. "More than Venice, Italy?"

"It's true." Gabi's expression shifted into that proud smile that appeared any time she discussed her hometown. Ainsley had noticed the reaction on more than one occasion lately. "I've never been to Venice, and I've never actually counted all the bridges here, but it's a fact they taught us back in elementary school—more of that Pittsburgh Pride I told you about the other night. It's part of our curriculum."

"That's pretty impressive," Ainsley conceded.

"If you liked that, how about this factoid—there are over seven hundred sets of public stairs within our city limits. We literally have an Inspector of Steps who is responsible for maintaining them."

"An interesting job," Ainsley said, but then reconsidered, "or maybe a really boring one. I guess I don't know what maintaining public stairs entails."

"Me neither. They never mentioned that part at school," Gabi confessed. "It wouldn't be my top career choice, but to each their own." Her smile faded. "Although, I might need a new career, so maybe I shouldn't rule anything out right now."

An uncomfortable silence stretched between them. Ainsley hated the way a black cloud seemed to settle over Gabi at the mention of her career. She especially hated that she technically had a hand in its tenuous state. Fortunately, as they pulled into the parking garage, Gabi seemed to recover, and she shifted back into Slice of Italy Committee business mode. Ainsley was grateful Gabi had the festival to focus on.

Once inside the building housing Health Spot headquarters, they found the appropriate bank of elevators and Gabi pressed the button for the forty-third floor.

"Geez, that seems high." Ainsley's stomach dropped as the elevator car began its ascent.

"And it's only two-thirds of the way to the highest floor. This is the tallest building in Pittsburgh."

Ainsley thought perhaps Gabi should be a tour guide for the city with all her knowledge of it, but bit back the comment. No need to bring up the shaky status of Gabi's employment status yet again.

The woman at the Health Spot front desk led them to Mr. Little's office, but the moment Ainsley spotted him, she realized something wasn't quite right. This man was young— late twenties, maybe early thirties. There was no way he was Vic's contact back in the '90s. Ainsley's heart sank. They had the wrong guy. She could tell by Gabi's furrowed brow that she was doing the math too and things weren't adding up for her either. This meeting couldn't go sideways—Gabi needed a win.

"You're here about the Bloomfield Slice of Italy Festival?" he asked once they'd exchanged pleasantries and they all had sat. "How can I help?"

"Well," Ainsley began cautiously. "To be honest, I'm not entirely sure you can. We were looking for the Charlie Little who partnered with the festival committee on behalf of Health Spot quite a few years ago. I'm guessing that wasn't you, and I'm very sorry we've wasted your time." She was even more sorry that she had wasted Gabi's time, not to mention getting her hopes up that they'd solved the festival's sponsorship.

"It wasn't you, was it?" The hopeful way Gabi's question hitched up at the end made Ainsley's heart hurt. She wanted so badly for the festival to succeed.

"I'm afraid it wasn't. I'm sorry." He sounded like he meant it. "That would've been my father. I am Charlie Little *Jr.* Dad worked here up until a few years ago. We lost him in the pandemic."

Both Ainsley and Gabi expressed their sympathies. Mr. Little nodded gravely in response before he spoke again. "My father grew up in Bloomfield and always loved the Slice of Italy

Festival. He would take me and my sister every year when we were kids. My grandparents lived there their whole lives."

Ainsley's ears perked up. This guy had ties to the festival. From the sound of it, cherished childhood memories. Perhaps all was not lost. She bumped her knee against Gabi's to telegraph her hope. "Mr. Little, did you know that your father acted as an advocate for the festival here at Health Spot, helping to secure much-needed funds for the event?"

"Please, call me Charlie," the young man interjected.

"The festival had to shut down back in 2020 due to the pandemic, and in the years right after, there was nobody at the helm to start it up again," Gabi chimed in. "With the help of some other business owners in Bloomfield, I'm getting it started again this summer. The Slice of Italy Festival has always been an important part of our neighborhood's culture. We can't lose that. It means a lot to me personally, but it also means a lot to our community. I'm sure you know Pittsburgh is a city that has always celebrated its neighborhoods and their diversity. I think it's important that we continue to do that. But to bring the festival back, we need sponsors, and since Health Spot had always been such a big supporter in the past, we were hoping they'd want to join us again. By any chance can you put us in touch with the individual here who could help us with that?"

Charlie leaned back in his chair and blew out a long breath. Was it a sigh of exasperation at the interruption of his workday? His gaze moved from Gabi, to Ainsley, before finally landing on a framed picture on his desk. His eyes brightened as he finally spoke. "I can do you one better than that." He full-on smiled at them. "I'd be happy to step in as the festival's new advocate here. I always loved going to Slice of Italy, and I want to share that with my kids too. I hadn't realized the event had shut down completely. I've been a little preoccupied." He angled the frame so they could see the image of him and his wife...and two little boys—possibly twins—around the age of three. "My dad never got the chance to meet these guys, and that weighs on my heart. Taking his place to help support the festival seems like a good way to honor him. Plus, I can bring back our family tradition of enjoying Slice of Italy every summer."

"Are you serious, Charlie? Could you do that?" Gabi clutched her hands in her lap as if forcing herself not to celebrate too soon.

"Absolutely." He gave a firm nod. "I'll put together a proposal and get it to the right people early next week. I should have confirmation a few days after that."

Gabi sprang from her chair and reached across the desk to shake his hand, relief etched on her face. "Thank you, Charlie. Thank you from me, the committee, and the neighborhood of Bloomfield."

* * *

Just in time for their shifts at D'Angelo's, Ainsley and Gabi walked into the restaurant arm in arm, still giddy from their fundraising success.

"As soon as I change my clothes I'll put the good news in the committee's group chat." Gabi grinned at her. "Don't worry, I'll totally give you all the credit for making the connection."

"Me? This victory was entirely yours."

"Let's call it a team effort," Gabi said, pulling Ainsley into a hug. "I couldn't have done it without you."

Their celebration was cut short when Jane hurried over to the two of them and stood like a blockade between them and the dining room.

"Ainsley," Jane said, her voice low and conspiratorial. "There's a woman from Gustare Foods here to see you. Linda, I think she said. She's been here for about fifteen minutes. I gave her some coffee and she settled in at a booth over there with her laptop." Jane tipped her head in the direction of the row of booths lining the wall where, just as she said, Linda was seated looking less than pleased.

Unannounced. This couldn't be a good sign.

"Thanks, Jane," Ainsley said as she desperately racked her brain as to what could have triggered this surprise visit and what could get it started off on the right foot. "Would you please go back to the kitchen and put in an order for a small charcuterie board?"

"And an order of artichoke dip," Gabi added as Jane bustled off. To Ainsley she said, "Brian's artichoke dip is the best. If you're trying to impress her with food, let's take our best shot. I'll be in the kitchen if you need me."

"Thanks." Ainsley gave her arm a squeeze, took a steadying breath, and headed over to the booth.

"Hello, Ainsley." Linda's voice held an uncalled for edge of animosity. "You're mighty dolled up for a day of restaurant work. Is it a special occasion?"

Ainsley took a beat before responding. This attitude from Linda was new, and her instinct was to tread lightly. There was no reason to reveal anything about her morning's activities—they had nothing to do with Gustare Foods. "We just made a trip into town. Nothing fancy. My work here in the restaurant is mostly front of house. I dress up often."

"Hmm. I see." Linda didn't sound convinced. "And who was your friend you came in with? Was that the D'Angelo girl you were hugging?"

There it was. "Gabriella D'Angelo. She's a hell of a chef, and she manages the kitchen like a total pro. She was supposed to take over the restaurant when her father retired."

"Yes, yes." Linda waved a dismissive hand. "I know about Miss D'Angelo. What I don't know is why you're cuddling up with the client. Care to enlighten me?"

Ainsley swallowed hard and willed her cheeks not to redden. It wasn't like Linda knew she and Gabi had spent the night together just a few nights earlier. Besides, nothing had happened that night other than sleeping. Well, mostly. Okay, a little mild making out. Not that she hadn't wanted more, it just hadn't been in the cards that day. Of course, there were those other incidents she hoped Linda never found out about…

"Ainsley?" Linda snapped her fingers to regain her attention.

Oh, right. "That was nothing. Gabi, uh, *Gabriella* had just received some good news and I was congratulating her. That's all." Despite her best efforts, she felt heat creeping up her face.

"I knew it," Linda said in a pitying tone, shaking her head. "You're getting attached. We talked about this, Ainsley. Getting too comfortable with the client is unacceptable. I'm concerned about your ability to complete this assignment."

Oh no. This was not happening now. Ainsley had remained completely professional throughout her time there so far. Well, for *most* of her time there so far, when she was in the restaurant. She had kept things with Gabi totally professional if there were other people around. Except for just then when they'd walked in and hugged it up in the middle of the dining room. While Linda was there. *Crap.*

"What? No. Everything here is going fine," Ainsley insisted. Luckily Jane delivered the charcuterie and dip to the table, providing a distraction. "Linda, why don't you finish your coffee, have something to eat, then I'll give you a tour of the place and show you firsthand just how great things are going here."

While Linda snacked, Ainsley made a beeline for the restroom and splashed some water on her face. She couldn't get pulled from the assignment and have that failure hanging over her head for the rest of her career with Gustare Foods. Or worse…would they fire her for something like this? She tried to remember what the employee handbook said about fraternization. It probably wasn't viewed in a positive light.

A surprise Gustare Foods inspection. Of all the freaking bad luck. *Pull yourself together.*

All she had to do was go out there and show Linda around. Operations really had been running smoothly in the past couple of weeks. Thanks to her endless checklists and side work charts, Ainsley had the whole front of house now following Gustare Foods' regulations. And since that day she and Gabi had discussed potential health-code violations, the kitchen had been on the straight and narrow as far as the rules went. They had all been working hard and it would pay off now. She looked her reflection in the eye. There was nothing to worry about.

After a few more deep breaths, she met Linda back in the dining room for the tour. Jane had stayed on after her shift would normally have ended without Ainsley asking her to do so and kept the afternoon staff in line. It was as if she was instinctively defending her territory. Ainsley could see why Gabi had always spoken so highly of her. She was so grateful for Jane in that moment, she could hug her—but she wouldn't risk further accusations of getting too familiar with the staff.

Linda began in the server station before meandering between the tables eyeing up the chairs, the floor, presumably anything that she could criticize. "I admit, this all looks shipshape out here," she said and Jane who had made herself busy wrapping silverware gave Ainsley a wink. "Now, let's see the kitchen."

Ainsley was confident Gabi and Brian would have everything in order, and as Linda moved through the kitchen making notes and consulting her own lists on her tablet, it certainly seemed they did not disappoint. Everything received approving, if not somewhat resentful, nods. Until Linda spotted the mason jars lined up on the steel prep table by the stove top. It appeared Gabi was preparing for another evening of canning.

"What is this?" Linda was incredulous, as if it was a row of singing rats there in the kitchen instead of jars. "Why have empty glass containers been left behind on a prep table? This is basically garbage just lying around. Somebody get these into the recycling bin please."

Gabi jogged over to join them. "Oh no, that's not recycling. They're clean and they're mine."

"No running in the kitchen," Linda barked and made another note on her tablet. "And what do you mean, *they're yours*? If they're yours, why are they here?"

Gabi looked surprised at the reprimand, but to her credit she responded calmly, "I'm doing a little canning after dinner service tonight."

"Here?" Linda frowned. "No. Absolutely not. You can take care of that hobby in your own kitchen. At home."

Gabi looked stricken. Ainsley witnessed the realization settle over her face. First to be told that she couldn't can her sauce at D'Angelo's, but also the harsh reminder that D'Angelo's kitchen didn't belong to her any more. Her jaw clenched like she was struggling to hold her emotions in check, but she remained silent.

"This isn't something she can do at home though," Ainsley piped up. She saw Gabi's eyes go wide, indicating she should stop talking, but she had to do something to help. "She's canning the sauce to sell it, so she needs to do it in an industrial kitchen to meet health-department guidelines."

Linda's lips had pursed as Ainsley spoke, and they finally separated with a moist smack. "You intend to sell sauce you're canning here somewhere else? No. You can't do that. It's a liability Gustare Foods isn't going to take on. This is your own personal business. Take it somewhere else."

Gabi, who had an angry vein throbbing in her temple, was already packing her jars back into their cardboard box as Linda stalked away.

"You're just packing it in?" Ainsley hissed. "Aren't you even going to try to fight for this?"

Gabi shook her head. "There's no use. It's Gustare Foods' call, not mine. It's bad enough they've taken the restaurant from me, and now this. There's no way in hell I want that bitch to know how badly she's beaten me down, and that's all that will happen if I go off on her. Screw that. Besides, I've got a festival problem to deal with now too. The oldies band that's supposed to be our headlining act just dropped out and we've got to find a replacement that will still draw people in. People in Pittsburgh love Classic Gold. We were really counting on them to bring in a crowd. We could really be screwed now. So, no. I've got no fight left in me for Gustare Foods today."

Ainsley blew out an exasperated breath before rushing out of the kitchen, chasing after Linda. "Linda, wait. What's the harm in letting her do this? Gabi's not canning during work hours. She's doing it on her own time. Can't she just use the kitchen after the dinner rush?"

Linda stopped walking so abruptly that Ainsley nearly crashed into her, and when she spun around the look on her face was positively venomous. "No. She cannot use the kitchen for her own personal canning operation. I don't know how to state this any more clearly. If I catch wind that this continues— or any other nonrestaurant business is happening here—you can kiss your job goodbye. It is your responsibility to be sure that woman ceases and desists. Do not let me and the company down."

"Linda—"

"I'm serious, Ainsley," she snapped. "Are you up to the task or not? Just tell me now."

Ainsley had to make it through this assignment—she couldn't face failure on the job. And it didn't seem like Gabi would want her to make a bigger scene than they already had. Maybe Gabi was right—Gustare Foods had won another round and there was nothing they could do about it. "I am. I'll make sure it doesn't happen again."

"Good." Linda's expression lost its sharp edge, but she still looked far from pleased. "I'm still not convinced you haven't become attached to the client, but based on my walk-through today, the restaurant has met all the Gustare Foods standards, so I don't have anything that would warrant you being written up. You can bet I'll be keeping a very close eye on you though, Ainsley. You'd better watch your every step for the remainder of this assignment."

CHAPTER TWENTY-ONE

Gabi spent the weeks after Gustare Foods shut down her canning operations living up to the obligations of their contract, but basically sleepwalking through her days. She went to work every day, barked orders in the kitchen and did all her required duties, then went straight home to the comfort of her couch, craving solitude and the escape of sitcom reruns on *Nick at Nite*. The only exceptions she'd made to this new routine were festival committee meetings and her visits to Nonna's on her Tuesday afternoons off work.

Today Nonna had her helping with outside chores—fixing a loose board on the back deck, cutting the lawn, weeding the flower beds. The physical strain felt supremely satisfying, and when she finally came inside for some shade and lemonade, and Nonna asked her to give her a hand with her laundry, she didn't mind in the slightest.

"Just carry the whole hamper downstairs for me," Nonna instructed. "I'll sort it into loads down there."

"Nonna, I can throw a load in for you. I know how to do laundry."

"Just carry it down," Nonna repeated. "Don't take an old lady's simple joy of being capable of doing laundry from me."

Gabi obeyed and carried the hamper down to the basement, but when she returned to the kitchen she slumped into the chair across from Nonna and blew out a long, pitiful sigh.

"What is going on with you, Gabriella?" Nonna refilled her lemonade. "You've had that same sad face on for weeks now. It's not your best look."

"Wow. If you can't count on your family to tell you the truth, who can you count on?" Gabi attempted a smile which she hoped would assuage Nonna's concern and possibly close the subject as well.

"I'm serious, nipotina. Talk to me."

Knowing Nonna would never betray her confidence, Gabi wasn't worried about the monetary consequences that came with breaking the nondisclosure clause in the Gustare Foods contract. She told her the whole story, including the most recent bit about Linda's surprise visit to D'Angelo's and how she'd put the nix on the sauce canning operation.

"It was supposed to be the activity that kept me busy until I opened a new restaurant or food truck or whatever else. Now I don't know what to do with myself," Gabi lamented. "I still have the jars from the first batch I canned if you want some."

"You put *my* sauce in a jar?" Nonna's face puckered like she was going to spit. "Sauce from a *jar?*"

"But it's your sauce, Nonna," Gabi argued. "It's the recipe we use at D'Angelo's."

"Nipotina, you're missing the whole point of homemade sauce. The point is that it's made from scratch, fresh. It's not the tomatoes or the spices—not the *ingredients* that make our sauce special, it's the love and the joy of feeding people and treating them to something delicious and comforting. You can't put that in a jar, and you can't pour it out of one."

"We've lost the restaurant, Nonna." Gabi's eyes stung with tears she blinked back. "The recipes are all I have left."

"All you have left." Nonna rolled her eyes. "So dramatic. You have everything you ever had. So you're going to lose a pile of bricks. It's not the end of the world. You can get another."

"But when and where?" Gabi hated the whine in her voice. "I feel so untethered."

"You'll figure all that out, but it's not something you can rush. It's like my sauce—sometimes things need to simmer a while for the magic to happen. This sauce-in-a-jar thing, is it really what you want anyway? It sounds to me like New York all over again. Don't waste your time on silly pursuits—work on your actual dream." She patted Gabi's hand. "In the meantime, don't you have a festival to organize?"

"Don't remind me." If Nonna was trying to use Slice of Italy to boost Gabi's spirits, she was making a misstep. There were only three weeks left until the festival weekend, and the committee had yet to fill the entertainment headliner slot left vacant by Classic Gold, the oldies group that had ducked out, claiming to be double-booked. The situation needed her attention. She blew out another long breath of surrender and admitted, "I guess you're right."

"You're doing a good thing bringing Slice of Italy back to Bloomfield. The festival was a special thing for us all—so many good memories associated with it. You're going to make a lot of people happy."

"I hope a lot of people are going to show up." If they didn't get a decent act for Saturday night, they may not. "We just have no way to predict what size crowd to expect."

"Ah, it's like that old baseball movie," Nonna said knowingly with a joking twinkle in her eye. "If you build it, they will come. It sounds like you've been gifted the time to put more effort into the festival. I would take advantage of that if I were you. Let the rest of the stuff simmer for a bit. Just like the sauce. What can it hurt?"

Nonna was right again, of course. But as Gabi sucked down the last of her lemonade, one thing Nonna said stood out in her mind. The memories people carried around with them of Slice of Italy were a strong force—she'd seen that when they'd talked with Charlie Little at Health Spot. She had even heard the same sentiment from Darrius at Danielle's house party.

Suddenly the solution to the festival's entertainment problem was clear to her. She hopped up and kissed Nonna on the top of her head. "Nonna, I think you just saved the day. Thank you." She put her empty glass in the sink. "I've gotta run."

"That's my nipotina!" Nonna called after her as she headed out the back door.

* * *

Gabi practically ran down the street to Danielle's house, but when she rang the bell, there was no response. With a quick text she discovered that even though it was her day off, Danielle was at D'Angelo's. *Weird.*

When she made it to the restaurant fifteen minutes later, Danielle wasn't behind the bar, but before Gabi could even ask Jane if she'd seen her, Danielle came through the swinging doors that led to the kitchen. *Even weirder.*

"Hey, there you are," Danielle practically sang the words as she linked their arms and guided Gabi toward the bar. "How about a beer? You look a little wilted. What have you been up to today?"

There was no doubt she was more than a little sweaty from working in the yard at Nonna's, but Gabi wasn't fooled by Danielle's babbling. "I'll take a Big Dog IPA. Why are you acting weird?"

"Me?" Danielle slid behind the bar and pulled two drafts. "I'm not weird. I'm merely asking about your day."

"I was helping out at Nonna's, and I had an idea." No time like the present to ask a friend for a favor. "We need a big act for Saturday night at Slice of Italy, and I remembered Darrius saying how much he loved the festival when he was a kid, and I thought maybe he would…"

"That he would come back with Sweaty Yeti and play a set," Danielle finished for her with a big smile. "I bet he'd love to. I'll give you his number and you can call him."

Danielle pulled her phone out of her pocket, but then something over Gabi's shoulder seemed to catch her attention. "Um, but first there's something you need to see in the kitchen."

"What?" Gabi twisted on her barstool to see what she was looking at, but it was only the swinging kitchen doors. "No, the sooner I get this settled, the better. What's his number?"

She shook her head as she stood. "Gabi, the call is going to have to wait. You're needed in the kitchen now."

Gabi slid off her seat and followed Danielle, still unsure what her friend was talking about. "I'm not even supposed to be here. What could they possibly need me for in the kitchen? If this is more Gustare Foods crap, I don't even want to hear it."

When they pushed through the doors, Gabi saw Ainsley standing outside her office and wearing paint-splattered coveralls together with a huge, beautiful grin. She struggled to make sense of the scene. Ainsley wasn't supposed to be working either. Why was she dressed like that? And what was so urgent that Gabi had to be rushed into the kitchen? She turned back to Danielle. "What is happening here?"

But Danielle gestured to Ainsley. "It was all her idea. I was just a helper bee."

"Surprise!"

Gabi spun around to see Ainsley giving sparkle hands.

"What surprise?" Gabi crossed the kitchen in a few long strides.

"This one." Ainsley threw open the office door to reveal the apparent fruits of her labor. "I know you'll only be using it for another month or so, but you should have the optimal experience while you do."

The office walls were no longer covered in the chipped mint-green paint. They were now a calm pewter gray. Even the old metal filing cabinet had been given a fresh coat of paint in a coordinating darker gray. Gabi stepped into the space to get a better look. Her industrial-grade chair with the wobbly wheel had been replaced by a modern ergonomic office chair, and the old bulletin board was now a whiteboard complete with magnets and dry-erase markers. Everything was fresh and new.

"Don't worry about all the papers you had tacked on the old board," Ainsley said hastily. "I didn't throw anything away. I tucked them all in a file in the cabinet in case you need or want them."

Gabi opened her mouth to respond, but found she was speechless. Ainsley had used her day off to redecorate the office? "You…did this?"

"I had some help." Ainsley shrugged. "I couldn't have done it without Danielle, and Brian did a lot of heavy lifting. Literally."

Gabi ran her fingers along the surface of the desk—the only item in the room that appeared unchanged, although there were now trays on it for the unruly stacks of paper invoices and mail that used to litter it. "But why?"

"Because you work really hard and the kitchen can be a really chaotic place. You deserve a space where you can get a minute of respite to collect your thoughts and handle all the behind-the-scenes stuff that a manager is responsible for." Ainsley hooked her thumbs in her front pockets and bounced slightly on her toes, clearly proud of her work. "And, let's face it, this office was in desperate need of a makeover."

"But the budget—I thought we were reining in expenses," Gabi blurted out. Ainsley had done something really thoughtful for her—on her day off, no less—and there she was questioning it. She could feel the silent words behind Danielle's sharp gaze, *just enjoy the gift, jagoff.* "I mean, thank you. This is incredible."

Ainsley let out a laugh, presumably at Gabi's change of direction. "You're welcome. And don't worry, with the impaired wheel on the old chair, replacing it was a matter of safety. Gustare Foods had no qualms about paying. The chair was the only pricey piece of the makeover, so I didn't bother to submit the can of paint and desk organizers. That's my gift to you."

"You paid for them yourself? Let me pay you—"

A shoulder bump from Danielle stopped Gabi from finishing the sentence. "Uh, I mean, thanks. This is a very kind gift. I love it."

"I'm glad." Ainsley's eyes were soft and filled with an inner glow. She was so beautiful in that moment, paint splatters and all, Gabi couldn't resist pulling her into a very grateful, strong hug right there in front of everybody.

CHAPTER TWENTY-TWO

Ainsley found the combination of the morning's hard work and Gabi's obvious pleasure quite satisfying. She had hoped her scheme to lift Gabi's spirits with an upgrade to the little office would not be taken as her overstepping any boundaries. She took the enthusiastic hug she received as a sign that the plan had worked.

She had the feeling that Gustare Foods, or perhaps Linda, was trying to punish them—Gabi, D'Angelo's Italian Restaurant, and Ainsley herself. It gave her an unshakable sense that something was wrong.

Ainsley didn't blame Gabi one bit for the way she had seemed to retreat from everything other than pure work obligations, but she sure didn't like it. They hadn't seen each other outside of D'Angelo's in weeks. She missed having Gabi show her around Pittsburgh. Additionally, Gabi had stopped popping into the restaurant outside of her scheduled work hours and when she was around she was in a strictly business mode. Ainsley found herself longing for the lively, boisterous way Gabi used to manage the kitchen. Lately she'd been more of the quietly commanding type—just ticking the boxes. Still effective, yet somehow lacking. But of course, that was completely understandable given the odious circumstance of losing her life's passion.

She had hoped the office makeover would jolt Gabi out of her gloomy mood and let them get back to enjoying the last bit of their time together.

She poured herself a glass of iced tea and waited for Gabi to finish her phone call to Darrius. Gabi's first order of business in her new office. Fingers crossed, it would be successful and maintain the good feeling.

"You and Gabi sure seem to be bosom buddies these days." Kelsey's smirk edged toward menacing as she crossed her arms and parked herself against the counter in the server station.

The bubbles of excitement in Ainsley's brain began to pop. Maybe it had been a mistake to be so openly friendly in the kitchen, but Gabi had hugged *her*, and who was Ainsley to deny the expression of gratitude? It was a thank-you—a totally normal gesture. Plus, after the distance that had drifted between them over the past couple of weeks, the contact had felt wonderful. Heat flushed Ainsley's cheeks. Just because Kelsey had used the phrase *bosom buddies* didn't mean she knew Ainsley was more than a little familiar with Gabi's bosom.

"She was just thanking me for…" Redecorating a coworker's office as a surprise did feel a little bosom buddy-like, so Ainsley redirected. Not that it was any of Kelsey's business anyway. "A kindness. It was no big deal. I aim to get along with all my coworkers. We're a team here."

"If you say so," Kelsey said with a sarcastic laugh and a toss of her dirty-blond hair.

Ainsley normally let Kelsey's dark attitude roll off her back, but today it was rubbing at her like an itchy wool sweater. How dare that kid try to harsh her happy vibe? "Kelsey, please tie back your hair before you serve any customers." Ainsley's reminder had a distinct all-business tone by design. "In fact, it should be tied back before you even come into the server station. This is considered a food service area just like the kitchen."

The reprimand was met with an eye roll, but it had its desired effect. Kelsey shuffled sullenly out of the station. And just in time for Gabi to come into the dining room with a victorious smile.

"He said yes!" she announced as she entered the server station.

"He said yes!" Ainsley repeated and grabbed Gabi's hand, hesitant to go full embrace again after Kelsey's comments. "We should celebrate with dinner tonight."

"We should," Gabi confirmed as she filled a glass with diet soda. "But it's my treat. To thank you for making my office a beauteous space."

"You already said thank you." Ainsley sipped her tea, and quickly added, "But I'd be happy to let you do so again."

"Great." Gabi smiled. "We can swing by your place so you can change out of your handywoman getup, then let's go grab a bite."

* * *

"You were right, this sandwich is life-changing," Ainsley said and licked a wayward drip of vinegary dressing from her finger. It was amazing how putting the french fries and slaw right on the sandwich made such a difference to her southwest bean burger.

"You've never put your side dishes directly on your burger before?" Gabi teased with a wink. She had pretty much devoured her roast beef sandwich, then picked up the shreds of cabbage that had dropped off it and popped them into her mouth. "I think the Italian bread they use makes it so good."

They were sharing a table in the outdoor seating area of the restaurant, enjoying the warm May day. Ainsley squinted against the sunshine and smiled as a family with three little boys in matching Hawaiian shirts all holding hands passed by on the sidewalk. A hint of the upcoming summer was in the air, and everyone out and about downtown that day seemed to feel it.

"Who knew Pittsburgh was such a foodie haven?"

"Are you kidding me?" Gabi mopped her face with a paper napkin and leaned back in her metal chair. "Pittsburgh is all about culinary delights. We're the birthplace of the Big Mac. We're the home of Heinz Ketchup and Turner's Iced Tea. Hell, we have person-sized pierogies run a foot race during the seventh-inning stretch at our ballpark."

"Well, color me corrected." Ainsley laughed. "And I'd really like to see that pierogi race thing."

"I'll take you to a ball game sometime," Gabi offered. "It's seriously a beautiful park."

"That sounds fun." Ainsley kept her smile firmly in place even as her mind calculated the time remaining on her assignment with D'Angelo's. The weeks had been flying by, which meant the days she had left for ball games and dinner dates with Gabi were limited. She wanted to make the most of them, but it sure was going to be hard to say goodbye when the time came. What could she do, though? She finally had the role at Gustare Foods she had been working toward for years. She wasn't close with her family like Gabi. And she didn't own a home like Gabi's yellow-brick two-story, or have neighbors or close friends like she did either. Her career was her whole life. Wherever Gustare Foods sent her when her time in Pittsburgh was done, that was where she would go.

Both she and Gabi had known that was how it would be when they had made the decision to see each other as long as Ainsley was in town. Gabi seemed to be dealing with it just fine. So, why was it getting harder for Ainsley to accept it with each date they went on?

CHAPTER TWENTY-THREE

It was the Thursday afternoon before the Slice of Italy Festival when Jane appeared in the kitchen's service window, her expression tight with concern. "Gabriella," she stage-whispered, her tone anxious. "We have a Code Gray out here. I repeat—a *Code Gray*." She was gone just as suddenly as she'd appeared.

"What did she say?" Ainsley's beautiful face screwed up in confusion. "What's a Code Gray?"

Gabi's mouth went dry as her gaze darted around the kitchen. Nothing was too out of control—this would be okay. Still, she could use a minute to tidy up. "Ainsley, I need you to get out there and help Jane stall."

"Stall what?"

"The health inspector," Gabi said as she placed her hands on Ainsley's shoulders and walked her to the swinging door. "Just stall. I'll explain later."

"You heard her, people." Brian clapped his hands together to rally the kitchen staff. "We've got a Code Gray. Look alive!"

"Dale, tie your apron," Gabi instructed as she cruised by the fryer station. Floor was dry and clear of any clutter that shouldn't be lying around. Good. Steam table looked neat. Totes and bins in the walk-in clearly labeled. Temperature on the mark. She ended her quick tour by grabbing an abandoned knife out of the sink. That was a good save. But as she heard Ainsley's voice getting closer to the service window, she knew this was it—either things were correct or they weren't. It was all in the inspector's hands now.

"Chef," Brian called to her from the grill. "We need you on the line. Just got two dining room slips in and a big take-out order."

Of course, the inspector would arrive just as dinner service started to kick into gear. They would want to see the kitchen in action. On her way back to the steam table she noticed a lidless Big Gulp cup of soda someone left unattended on the prep table. Without a second thought she grabbed it and dropped it in the trash bin. Someone might be mad about it, but it was better than Gabi having to write them up for a health-code violation.

Gabi slid into her spot in front of the service window right as Ainsley and the inspector came through the swinging doors. She was grateful for the distraction of the meal slips clipped to the board—she would focus on her job and not pay the inspector any attention. Lifting the lid from each of the metal trays on the table in front of her, she confirmed everything was where she liked it to be when she was working the window. A quick glance around the kitchen showed all employees engaged in their duties. She hardly even noticed the inspector eyeing the board where OSHA and other mandatory information was posted. Instead, she simply stirred the gravy in the tray in front of her, then carefully replaced the ladle and lid to keep the heat in.

"Mr. Callaghan," Ainsley cooed at the inspector. "Before we go over to the *fryer station*, why don't you pop back in here and check out our dishwashing area since it's tucked back in the corner. Keep you from having to double back."

Mr. Callaghan seemed agreeable—who could deny Ainsley when she batted those long lashes at them—but her request made no sense. He would inevitably circle back. There was no getting around it—he would check out every inch of that kitchen, possibly even twice. And why had Ainsley said *fryer station* in that goofy tone? She'd put all the emphasis on the r's and made it sound very Pittsburghese. But Ainsley didn't have the Pittsburgh accent like the rest of them. It was almost as if she was trying to alert Gabi to something over at the…geez!

Not a second too soon Gabi spotted the spray bottle of cleaning solution sitting on the sliver of counter space between the deep fryer and the cooktop. In one swoop she slid down the line, grabbed the bottle, and returned it to the shelf away from the food where it belonged. She was back at her spot smiling sweetly—nothing to see here—when Ainsley and the inspector emerged from the dish room.

As they continued on their way, Gabi blew out a long breath. Time to focus on the orders continuing to trickle in from the dining room. There was nothing else to do about the inspector now but wait for his visit to pass.

* * *

"A couple of dings, but that's not so bad, right?" Ainsley ran a finger down her tablet's screen, scrolling through the report from the health inspector.

Gabi accepted the IPA Danielle passed across the bar and took a long drink. What a freaking night. The inspector showing up had put everybody on edge for the dinner service, and between in-house guests and take-out orders, it had ended up being especially busy. At least, as Ainsley had pointed out, there were no serious infractions, just a few missed points for the handwashing sink not heating to one hundred degrees quickly enough and a measuring scoop left in a sugar bin.

She lifted her glass in Ainsley's direction. "Thanks mainly to you."

"And to the whole staff here," Ainsley added. "If everyone hadn't done their part and listened when we went over those checklists earlier, this could've been much worse."

They had survived the visit. That was the important thing, although there was one question that had been ticking in the back of her mind from the moment Jane had given the Code Gray alert. "I wonder what triggered the Health Department to send someone out here. Didn't you say they usually only do that if they receive a formal complaint?"

Ainsley nodded as she swallowed another mouthful of wine. It seemed the evening had taken a toll on her as well. "That's right. Have we had any customer complaints lately that you know of?"

"Nothing," Gabi confirmed. "Nothing up front?"

"Nope."

"So, just a call directly to the Health Department," Gabi muttered against the rim of her tumbler of beer. "That's weird."

"Agreed. Unless…" Ainsley's expression darkened for a moment, but then she shook her head as if dismissing the thought. "You know what? All's well that ends well is what we should call this. And I've been dying to ask—why do you call it a 'Code Gray'?"

Gabi stifled a giggle at the term Jane had made up years ago. "What color was the inspector's suit?"

"Gray—" Understanding washed over Ainsley's face. "Ah, I get it."

"It always is." Gabi shrugged. "Plus, in hospitals when they call a Code Gray, it's because someone is displaying combative or aggressive behavior, and to me there is nothing more aggressive than some stranger coming into my kitchen and nebbing around."

Ainsley laughed but shook her head. "That is not at all the same thing."

"Well, it beats the old method of Jane screeching, 'health inspector!' through the service window." Gabi grinned. "That tended to freak out the customers."

"Understandable." Ainsley stood and straightened her skirt. Her shift was over, so she would have no reason to stick around unlike Gabi who still had a few odds and ends to tie up after the crew finished cleaning the kitchen. "I'm beat. I'm going to head out."

Gabi turned her back to the bar, hoping to avoid being overheard. "Any chance you want to meet up after I finish up here? I feel like we should be celebrating. If you don't want to go out, I could grab a bottle of wine and come to your place. The guys cleaning in the kitchen should be done soon."

Ainsley's plump lips formed an apologetic pout. "I'd love to, Gabi, but I think I'm going to have to take a raincheck on that." She held up her tablet. "I need to go over these results again and then put together my report for Gustare Foods."

Damn Gustare Foods. On top of everything else, they were beaver-damming her now. "Raincheck," she reluctantly agreed.

After they'd said good night and Ainsley left for the night, Danielle pulled them each another IPA draft and came around the bar to join Gabi for a drink. "You wanna talk about this, or what?" Danielle asked.

"Aw, I'm fine." Gabi waved a dismissive hand in her friend's direction. Now on the other side of it, the inspection no longer bothered her. They'd passed, and now it was back to business as usual, or at least as usual as business was under the watchful eye of Gustare Foods. She had three more weeks before they took over completely—she had to keep her focus on moving forward. "Can't let a little visit from the Health Department get you down."

"I'm talking about whatever this thing is that is going on between you and Ainsley."

"What?" A blatant stalling technique. Gabi wasn't sure she wanted to get into it.

But apparently she didn't have a choice. Danielle was her best friend and could read her too well. Plus she would never let her off the hook on something like that. "Don't even try it. You may have turned your back to me, but I heard you get served a raincheck despite your smooth moves." She pulled a face. "Seriously, I've seen the way you look at that woman. You love her."

Love? "Whoa, I don't know about that." Sure, she had feelings for Ainsley. They had fun whenever they hung out. And there was no denying the chemistry between them—that was evident from that first night together. But there was the one big concern that persisted in tugging annoyingly at her heart, keeping its protective walls firmly in place. "Ainsley won't be in town much longer. As soon as her assignment is complete, she'll leave. It's silly to try to start something serious. It doesn't make any sense."

Gabi swallowed hard against the sudden lump in her throat. Of course, she knew all along that Ainsley's time in Bloomfield was temporary, but there was something about saying it out loud that made it very real. And for some reason, at that moment, that made her very sad.

"The only silly thing about it is that you're being too stubborn to give a good thing a chance," Danielle said with an arched eyebrow that dared Gabi to argue with her. "Ainsley's a good one. If I were you, I wouldn't let her get away that easily."

"Ainsley *is* a good one—I completely agree." Gabi sighed. Ainsley would be gone, and so would D'Angelo's. It made her heart heavy to even think about it. "But she's also a company gal. Her job is everything to her, and Gustare Foods will keep her hopping from city to city. She's going to go where they send her. Not stay put here in Bloomfield."

"I'm just saying you should think about it. It's obvious you like her, and I've never known you to give up on something you want. You shouldn't let her job get in your way." Danielle gave her shoulder a comforting squeeze. "Speaking of jobs, I guess we should wrap things up here."

"Agreed." Gabi stood and stretched. *Back to it.* She would be much more motivated to check on the kitchen close if it meant she would be heading to Ainsley's instead of going home alone. Damned Gustare Foods. Maybe Danielle was right—maybe she should stop letting Gustare Foods get in her way.

CHAPTER TWENTY-FOUR

Ainsley poured a much-needed coffee and opened her laptop. She hadn't lied to Gabi the night before—she'd spent a couple of hours reviewing the inspector's report and completing the appropriate Gustare Foods forms. Meanwhile, she would have much rather spent the night sharing that bottle of wine with Gabi and whatever naturally followed. It figured, as soon as they finally got things back on track between them, the freaking health inspector showed up and left Ainsley saddled with a boatload of work that kept her holed up at home crossing t's and dotting i's for Gustare Foods.

But as she had run through it all, she couldn't stop wondering about what had triggered the inspection in the first place. Gabi had confirmed it—there had been no obvious customer complaints. Plus, in the couple of months she had been there, operations had been running more cleanly and efficiently. All the Gustare Foods standards had been implemented—she had made sure of that. What reason would there be for someone to make a complaint that warranted a visit from the Health

Department? She had tossed and turned all night trying to wrap her head around it, and when she'd finally managed to nod off, it hadn't lasted. She was wide awake before the sun had even thought about making an appearance on the horizon. Hence the second cup of coffee.

There was one explanation that would make all the pieces fit—the one she had nearly blurted out the night before over drinks with Gabi and Danielle. But there was just no way it could be true. She bit the inside of her lip and mentally ran through every interaction with Linda leading up to that point.

From the very start Linda had expressed her doubts about Ainsley's ability to complete the assignment at D'Angelo's. And when Ainsley had attempted to help Bruno get out of the contract, Linda had said it was either D'Angelo's business or Ainsley's job. But even after Ainsley had expressed her commitment to Gustare Foods, Linda still had her doubts and latched on to the idea that Ainsley was getting too close to the client. She basically implied that she couldn't treat the D'Angelo family with kindness and respect *and* do her job properly. The D'Angelo family, the staff at the restaurant, and the community had embraced her as one of their own from day one. Linda had even gone so far as to drop in unexpectedly to check on things— the day she had shot down Gabi's sauce canning operation in the kitchen. Then, just a few weeks later, the health inspector had shown up. It was just a little too convenient.

She couldn't wait any longer. It was after eight a.m. She deserved some answers.

As she waited for Linda to pick up, she hardened her resolve—she wouldn't be intimidated by Linda. Not this time. The D'Angelo's assignment was Ainsley's, and she had done a damned good job at it. She had nothing to regret.

"Ainsley, what a surprise," Linda said when she finally answered, but her tone wasn't surprised, more droll than anything. "Aw, did the visit from the Health Department not go as you'd hoped?"

A sour taste rose in Ainsley's throat. She hadn't uploaded her report about the visit yet, but clearly Linda was already aware that it had occurred. Ainsley's suspicions from the night before had been correct. "It was you," she managed. "You logged the complaint and that's how you know the inspector was at the restaurant yesterday."

"Don't be ridiculous, Ainsley. I mean, yes, I did make the complaint to the Health Department. But I only know you had the inspection yesterday because Kelsey told me."

"Kelsey?" Ainsley's mind reeled. Kelsey, the server at D'Angelo's had been speaking with Linda? Why? "How do you know Kelsey?"

"I placed her at D'Angelo's a couple weeks before you started. I needed someone there to keep me abreast of your progress, or potentially your lack thereof." Linda's voice dripped with disdain. "Imagine if she hadn't advised me on how chummy you and Miss D'Angelo had become. It was my understanding that you'd sworn off workplace romances. Isn't that why you ended what we had?"

There it was—the missing piece clicked into place for Ainsley. "This was all because you wanted to strike back at me for what happened between us? Like, some kind of revenge?"

"I want you gone, Ainsley." Her voice was brass-tacks hard now. "How can I leave you in the past when you're still at Gustare Foods? I thought maybe you would leave the company on your own—eventually take a better position elsewhere, but you just kept moving up through the ranks. I had no choice but to take matters into my own hands."

"Are you telling me you've been sabotaging me from the start of this assignment?"

"Well, not the start exactly." Linda's voice seemed to lose a bit of its edge, like she was reveling in the details of her plan finally being revealed. "It was dumb luck that the old man didn't understand what he was agreeing to when he signed the contract with Gustare Foods. That gave me the crack I needed to wedge into and put the pressure on you. And I tried to give you an easy out at the time, but you refused to simply resign. You just couldn't stand to fail at an assignment."

"So you decided to help me fail."

"Don't give me too much credit. First Kelsey told me how friendly you were getting with the client, and then when I came out there I saw you were allowing unsanctioned business activity like sauce canning on premises. How could I be sure that you would stick with the Gustare Foods directives after that?" She feigned innocence. "So I made a little call to the Health Department and suggested D'Angelo's could have a cleanliness issue in the kitchen. I thought maybe a visit from them would weaken your resolve to see this job through. And if the inspector had actually found an issue, then I would have the evidence I needed to show Gustare Foods you were incompetent and needed to be dismissed from employment. After all, who is the company going to listen to—me, an established employee who has worked for them for almost twenty years, or some newbie field consultant who has clearly made more than a few missteps along the way?"

After the years she'd put in with the company, working her way up the ranks, tackling each position with hard work and dedication, and being a loyal employee, this would all come down to a she-said/she-said situation with the deck stacked in Linda's favor simply because she'd been with the company longer. It sucked, but Linda was right.

"You'd planned to sabotage my assignment."

"Like I said, you certainly made it easy," Linda purred. "And what a boon for me that you had to deal with the hot mess that is Miss D'Angelo stepping in to replace her father on top of everything else that comes with managing a Gustare Foods takeover."

The muscles in Ainsley's jaw tensed and she ground her teeth, certain that steam must be pouring out of her ears cartoonlike. Gabi might be obstinate, headstrong, and loud, but she knew how to cook and manage a kitchen. Nothing about her was a hot mess. So what if she questioned authority and believed in her family traditions above all else? That didn't make her a mess, it made her…quite wonderful really. It was just too bad that Linda and Gustare Foods didn't see it that way. Just like they probably wouldn't see what a kick-ass job Ainsley had been doing for them all along.

She had made a mistake at the beginning of her career with them, and now it was coming back to haunt her. Linda may have been pushing the issue, but Ainsley had no one to blame but herself. As long as she was working for Gustare Foods, Linda would always be lurking in the shadows, just waiting for the chance to take her down and finally get her revenge at Ainsley ending their clandestine office affair and threatening to make it public. Losing her job was a high price to pay for the mistake she'd made by getting involved with Linda, but being free of it once and for all might be worth it.

In that instant, Ainsley knew what she had to do. Her heart hammered, but somehow she felt a lot lighter than she had when she started the conversation. "Linda, remember when you said you would let the D'Angelos out of the Gustare Foods contract if I resign? Did you actually mean that?"

"Of course," Linda replied. "Like I said, I want you gone. If that's what it take to be rid of you finally, we call off the contract, you take the blame and the fall, and lose your job. I go on at Gustare Foods as if the whole thing never even happened—like *we* never happened."

"You'll have my notice in your inbox as soon as we end this call and I get that agreement in writing. I officially resign."

CHAPTER TWENTY-FIVE

Gabi was only scheduled to work through lunch on Friday to give herself time to get to the festival site and help the rest of the committee set up for Slice of Italy, but as she went through her morning prep routine, Danielle's words from the night before ran on a loop in her brain. *You're being too stubborn to give a good thing a chance.* Was that what was happening? She saw it more as guarding her heart.

Ainsley loved her job—that had been obvious from day one with her checklists and rules—and she was really good at it too. There was still no doubt in Gabi's mind if Ainsley hadn't pushed the staff so hard to implement all the health and safety regulations, they wouldn't have passed that inspection. Did she have feelings for Ainsley? Of course. But her job kept her moving from place to place, and Gabi would never want to hold Ainsley back from doing something she loved.

She had just added the mini meatballs to the minestra maritata when Ainsley came into the kitchen through the back door. "Hey," Gabi greeted her. "Are you ready to experience your first Slice of Italy Festival? We can head over together after lunch to help with setup."

"Oh, I'm uh…I'm going to have to just meet you there later," Ainsley said with her eyebrows scrunched together in something that looked a lot like concern. She clearly had more on her mind than just the festival. "In fact, I'm just popping in now to let you know Gustare Foods is dissolving the contract with D'Angelo's. They reconsidered your dad's appeal."

The pot lid in Gabi's hand slid out of her grasp and clattered against the floor. She must have misheard—Gustare Foods was letting them out of the contract? Her heart pounded. D'Angelo's belonged to her family again. "What? Why would they…what?"

The sweet smile that took over Ainsley's face was reassuring. She looked genuinely happy for Gabi. "Yes, they reconsidered. The contract is null and void. You should have an email confirming it and, of course, you'll receive official documents to sign and close it out as well." Then sadness crept back into her expression. "And that means my time here at D'Angelo's is done. No more Business Management Barbie looking over your shoulder all the time. I'm sure it will be quite a relief."

Gabi knew it was a joke meant to lighten their impending goodbye, but her elation deflated. No Gustare Foods at D'Angelo's anymore meant no Ainsley at D'Angelo's. That wasn't supposed to happen for another two weeks. "You're done here?"

Ainsley nodded. "Gustare Foods is pulling out, effective immediately. My work here is done." She blinked a few times before giving a brave smile. "You'll be fine. D'Angelo's has come a long way in the past few months. The restaurant is ready for you to take over as manager. That's what you wanted, right?"

Of course, that was what Gabi had wanted—what she'd been waiting for. Her mind yanked back to her father's retirement party and how shocked—and hurt—she had been. But those disappointments had brought Ainsley to the restaurant—and into her life. Now maybe there was something that Gabi wanted other than just to take over the family business. But if she was understanding what Ainsley was saying, then—"But, you're leaving?"

"My assignment has been terminated." Ainsley chewed on her bottom lip as if choosing her words carefully. "Actually, my time at Gustare Foods has come to an end. I need to find a new job."

"They fired you?" Gabi felt a flash of anger heat its way up her neck. "That's bullshit. Because of a few dings on the health inspector's report?"

"No, it wasn't really about that," Ainsley insisted.

"Those jagoffs. Do they not know how good you are at what you do? The way you came in here and whipped this place into shape, but still treated everyone with respect and kindness." It was true—Ainsley had really made a difference at D'Angelo's, and in Gabi's life in general. She grabbed her hand. "I didn't know how badly we needed your help. You were exactly the kick in the ass we needed. And I'm grateful for that."

"I've been upgraded from pain in the ass to kick in the ass," Ainsley mused. "I'll take it."

"I'm serious." Gabi didn't understand why Ainsley was joking about the situation when she should be mad as hell. How could they fire her? "You've done an exceptional job here, and they don't even care. They can't just—"

"Gabriella, it's fine." Ainsley seemed adamant about shutting down the topic.

"It's not fine," Gabi insisted, but Ainsley held up her palm and halted further argument.

"There's something I need to tell you. Something I probably should have told you much sooner, but I really didn't think it would impact you or my time at D'Angelo's," Ainsley began. "When I first started working with Gustare Foods, I got into a romantic relationship with Linda, despite the fact that she was my superior at the company. It started as a result of some late nights at the office and my admiration of her status in the corporation and snowballed from there. But the more I got to know Linda, the more I realized she wasn't a very nice person and certainly not someone I wanted to be with, so I broke it off."

"You were with Linda?"

"It was a terrible mistake. And when I broke up with her, Linda was aggrieved. No, more than just aggrieved—more like insanely enraged. She's not really accustomed to people saying no to her, especially at work. She threatened to sack me. I threatened unfair dismissal. It could have become very nasty, lawyers, HR, being outed, and everything, but Linda eventually backed off and I thought that was the end of it. But apparently she's been waiting like a spider in a web for an opportunity to get her revenge. And my assignment here turned out to be it. I spoke to her this morning, and she admitted as much. Long and short of it is, I'm no longer employed by Gustare Foods, and I'm now desperately in need of a job. So, I'm going to stay with my folks in Florida for a bit while I figure out my next move."

Gabi felt like her brain was buffering—stuttering to keep up with reality. Ainsley's past involvement with Linda was a surprise, but she didn't care that it had happened. Who didn't have a blip in their personal romantic history they wished they could delete? Gabi could totally relate after her own experience with Hannah. But now Ainsley was done working for the company and moving on…to Florida? "You're going to Florida?" She wasn't prepared for Ainsley's time to come to an end so abruptly. And secretly she had been hoping all along that Ainsley's next Gustare Foods assignment would be somewhere local. Or at least somewhere closer to Pittsburgh than Florida. But there was no next Gustare Foods assignment, so that was that. "Today?"

"Tomorrow," Ainsley confirmed. "So, I'm going to go back to Ruby's and pack, then tie up a few loose ends. I'll meet you tonight for dinner at Slice of Italy."

"But the event lasts all weekend," Gabi said stupidly, as if Ainsley didn't already know that. Obviously, she had made her choice and it wasn't the Slice of Italy Festival, nor was it Gabi. "After all your hard work, you're going to miss it."

"I have no job, and I need to start looking for one right away." Ainsley's eyes went so wide that the white showed around the whole iris. It seemed like unemployment was kicking up anxiety for her. "At least I can enjoy the festival tonight. We can have one last date before I leave."

She had her brave face on again. As excited as Gabi had been about the festival, a big part of that feeling was the anticipation of sharing it with Ainsley and now…well, at least they had one last night together. It was no secret that work was the most important thing to Ainsley. Gabi wasn't surprised she was wanting to get right back to it. "Okay, then it's a date—dinner at the festival."

With a quick hug and a peck on the cheek, Ainsley rushed out the back door of the kitchen. Gabi found a clean pot lid for the soup and went back to her morning prep routine. Maybe if she kept moving the ache in her heart would subside.

* * *

It was just about an hour later—right before lunch service started—that Kelsey came through the swinging door from the dining room and returned Ainsley's departure to the front of Gabi's mind.

"I guess Ainsley told you." Kelsey looked even more surly than usual.

Why was Kelsey talking about Ainsley, and how did she even know already that she was done working at D'Angelo's? "Told me she's leaving?"

"Well, yeah." Kelsey shifted her weight from one foot to the other. "And about me too."

"You?" Gabi shook her head. She was having a challenging time keeping up with conversations. Jane stuck two meal checks in the service window, and she realized she didn't have time to stand there and puzzle it out. "Kelsey, I'm going to need you to just say what you're trying to say. The lunch rush is starting, and obviously we're shorthanded in the first place without Ainsley."

"That's what I'm talking about," she mumbled and looked down at her tennis shoes. "Since Ainsley resigned from Gustare Foods they've terminated my assignment here."

What the hell did Kelsey have to do with Ainsley's job? None of this made any sense to Gabi, and she was in no mood to try and guess. "Kelsey," she said with a little more bark in her voice than she intended. "I'm going to need you to expand on that."

"I only took the job here because I was hired by some lady named Linda at Gustare Foods to report back on Ainsley's progress. And now that she's no longer working here, they don't need me anymore. I assume since you know now that I was basically spying on Ainsley that you're going to let me go too. But the truth is, I really like working here, and I'd like to stay on if you'll have me. I mean, I know you're probably pissed off that I put that spray bottle of cleaner in the work area by the fryer during the inspection, but I only did it because I was told to by Gustare Foods. I was following orders. And I'm sorry."

"You were hired by some lady at Gustare Foods? Linda?" The same Linda that Ainsley had previously been in a relationship with? The more Gabi heard, the more questions she had. She rubbed her throbbing temples. Kelsey was placed at D'Angelo's by Gustare Foods to report back to headquarters on Ainsley's performance. That right there was pretty crappy. But then they had Kelsey attempt to sabotage the visit by the Health Department. That most likely explained the complaint made to the department in the first place. *Those jagoffs.* "And now that they're done with you, you want to continue to work here."

"Please." Her usual dour expression was now more pleading. Surprisingly, there was a sweetness in those charcoal-lined eyes when she wasn't scowling. "I'm really sorry about what I've done."

"We've got another check here," Brian growled from the service window. A not-so-subtle hint for Gabi to get back to the job.

"Wait." Gabi remembered something else Kelsey had said that didn't make sense. "Did you say Ainsley resigned? I thought she was fired."

"No. She definitely resigned." Kelsey frowned. "It was part of the deal—Gustare Foods dissolved the contract with

D'Angelo's, but Ainsley had to resign. I guess Linda wanted her to own up to her failure on the job."

Ainsley gave up her job so Gabi and her family could keep the restaurant? That couldn't be right. Ainsley's job was everything to her. And she had in no way been a failure at her job. Everything about this was totally bogus.

"Gabi, I am not fucking around," Brian yelled finally, out of patience with trying to hold down the kitchen without her. "Get your ass over here. Let's go."

"Okay," Gabi said, giving Kelsey's shoulder a squeeze. "Thanks for being honest with me."

"Does that mean I can stay?" It was quite possibly the first time Kelsey had smiled while at the restaurant.

"Yeah." Gabi nodded. "And you better get out there—sounds like Jane could use another set of hands in the dining room."

"Thanks, Gabi."

"But, Kelsey, if you ever leave cleaner in a food-safe area of the kitchen again, I'll have to write you up."

"Fair," she acknowledged before practically skipping out of the kitchen.

While Brian grumbled something about it being time she got to work, Gabi slid into her spot at the grill and pulled the items needed to fulfill the waiting checks. Sorting out her feelings about everything she had just learned about Ainsley and Gustare Foods would have to wait until the lunch rush passed.

CHAPTER TWENTY-SIX

Ainsley had managed to hold her tears in until she was safely back in her own place. Linda had been right about one thing—she had become attached to Gabi and to D'Angelo's. It broke her heart to have to leave, but now she had to look for something new, so the plan to live with her parents while she regrouped and mapped out her next career steps had been born. It made good economic sense to save on rent since she was unemployed, even if it meant retreating to Florida. Besides, why would Gabi want to have any sort of relationship with her now that she knew she had once been involved with Linda?

She hastily packed a suitcase. The quicker she finished, the sooner she could get to the Slice of Italy Festival and spend some time with Gabi. She didn't regret for one minute her decision to resign. The look on Gabi's beautiful face when she learned the contract had been dissolved and D'Angelo's would stay in her family was worth it alone. But regardless, as she learned more about Gustare Foods' business practices it had become clear that she couldn't be part of their company. While she loved the work, she believed in fair dealing and conducting business honestly, ethics her father had instilled in her from a very young age.

Pulling an empty duffel bag from under her bed, she began transferring the contents of her dresser into it—all but the outfit she would wear to travel the next day and a Pittsburgh Pirates T-shirt to sleep in later that night.

The T-shirt, she realized, belonged to Gabi. She had borrowed it the day Gabi had made spaghetti carbonara, and she'd never returned it. Having something personal of Gabi's felt comforting, a connection. It was silly really—they were connected because they had spent nearly every day together for the past two and a half months, working and sometimes just doing things together because they enjoyed each other's company. The dread about saying goodbye later that night was growing. She had nearly run out of D'Angelo's after sharing the news with Gabi because she was afraid she would melt into a blubbering fool right there in the middle of the kitchen, and she had sworn to herself she would remain composed and professional to the very end. She would also find a way to hold it together when it was time to really say goodbye.

Suddenly, she felt like the walls of the bedroom were closing in on her and she had to sit on the edge of her bed and focus on simply breathing. What if she couldn't find another job? She could only squat in her folks' retirement-community guest room for so long. And then what?

"Ainsley." Ruby's voice came from downstairs. "Are you up there?"

"Come on up," Ainsley managed between gasps. Maybe she should open a window and let some fresh air in.

"Are you okay?" Ruby finally appeared in the doorway. "You look white as the bedsheets."

"I'm just…" She sucked in air. "I think I'm having a little bit of a panic. I don't know."

"Oh, my dear." Ruby's eyes were full of concern as she shuffled over and sat next to her on the bed. She waved one hand rapidly in front of Ainsley's face to fan her. "Deep breaths, honey. You're okay."

Ruby continued to murmur encouraging words, her tone warm and comforting like a cup of her tea. Eventually Ainsley calmed down enough to relay the events that led to her resignation and consequently, her decision to leave Bloomfield.

"Ah, so you're going home to the comfort of family." Ruby nodded. "That's understandable."

"It's not exactly like that. I mean, my parents are great people. My father is the one who taught me to work hard, play fair and to treat others with respect. And my mom is just so full of kindness, she always stressed the importance of grace in serving others." Ainsley shifted on the bed and tucked one leg under her. "But I'm pretty embarrassed to be moving back with them, jobless and with no prospects. I feel like a total failure."

"A failure?" Ruby squinted at her in confusion. "You didn't sound like a failure in the story you just told me. You sounded like someone who stood up for themselves and for their friends, and someone who refused to treat others unfairly. There's nothing that says *failure* in any of that."

Heat burned in Ainsley's cheeks. "But I'm unemployed and have no idea what I'm going to do next. Quitting Gustare Foods might have ruined my career in business management. I don't know what else to do."

"Instead of hiding out in Florida, you could stay here and figure it out," Ruby suggested gently. "I know one woman who would be happy if you did."

"Gabi?" Ainsley shook her head. "She's going to be busy running D'Angelo's. I'm really happy for her—it's what she always wanted. I can't be a distraction to that. Plus, I told her something today that might change her mind about wanting to be involved with me at all."

Ruby patted Ainsley's knee. "You know, I've never known Gabriella D'Angelo to let other people tell her what she wants— she likes to decide that on her own. Why don't you give her a chance to decide?"

Could she really be a part of what Gabi wanted? This time when Ainsley's pulse picked up, it wasn't the result of panic, it was excitement. Was staying in Bloomfield while she figured out her next step really a possibility? Could she live with the regret if she didn't at least try? "I guess that seems fair."

"Good," Ruby said, pushing up from the bed. "And by the way, I love having you here too. I'll meet you downstairs."

Ainsley's chest filled with warm comfort, a feeling she had been experiencing more frequently the longer she stayed in Bloomfield. Another plus in the "pro" column for sticking around. "For tea and cookies?"

"Oh no, child. We don't want to ruin our appetites when we're about to have the best Italian food in the 'Burgh." Ruby grinned. "We're going to the Slice of Italy Festival."

* * *

Ainsley found plenty more to put in the *Stay In Bloomfield* "pro" column when they arrived at the festival. When they turned the corner onto Liberty Avenue, the sight was outstanding. Several blocks of the road had been shut down to traffic and were lined with vendor tents. Some of them represented the businesses behind them, others sponsored by businesses from outside Bloomfield that had come in just to take part in the celebration. There was also a section lined with food trucks offering everything from specialty coffees to chicken-on-a-stick to funnel cakes. Hundreds of people—young and old alike— were milling around enjoying the sights and sounds of the Italian celebration. A band was playing accordion-heavy Italian folk music on the festival stage. In front was a large cluster of picnic tables, and it was there that they found the members of the Monday afternoon card club.

Vic stood as they approached and immediately pulled Ainsley into a hearty embrace. "Ainsley, I'm so glad you decided to join us. We heard you were leaving town and were worried you wouldn't make it to the festival tonight. We also heard you stood up to a corporate bully, brave girl." He beamed at her as they finally drew apart. "What? Don't look so surprised. News travels fast in the neighborhood."

It wasn't the rate at which the news had traveled that had caused Ainsley's surprise, it was more about Vic's words. He called her *brave girl*. He was proud of her, which for some reason made her head buzz with joy. But still, she couldn't help wondering what had been said about her parting ways with Gustare Foods? And by whom? She barely had time to mull it over before Ida pulled her down onto the bench and slid a plastic cup of red wine in front of her.

"Oh well…" Ainsley stammered, as she tried to find an appropriate response. "I don't know if I really did all that much."

"And, maybe she's leaving, maybe she's not," Ruby said cryptically as she gingerly settled into a spot at the table. "Let's just enjoy the festival. Ida, pass me one of those cups of wine."

"I heard you saved D'Angelo's." Ida passed a cup down the table.

"I heard that Gabi said they would've never been ready for the visit from the inspector if you hadn't been on board the past two months," Gerri, wearing her Italian flag T-shirt, joined in. "But I also heard the inspector was called in under false pretenses because together you and Gabi had that restaurant running like a fine-oiled machine."

"Oh no," Ainsley protested between sips of delicious wine. "It's Gabi who is the heart of D'Angelo's and keeps the machine chugging along. I just…helped."

"Well, there's no denying that the two of you make a great team," Ruby said before emptying her glass in one last gulp.

"And there's no denying Bloomfield is better for having you with us." Vic patted Ainsley's back.

Maybe there were more reasons than just Gabriella D'Angelo for Ainsley to stick around in Bloomfield. And maybe a relationship with her was worth a try too—if Gabi would even still consider it after learning about her past involvement with someone as obviously despicable as Linda.

CHAPTER TWENTY-SEVEN

"You did it." Danielle grinned at Gabi as they walked along Liberty Avenue arm in arm. "Look at all these people. Slice of Italy is back and better than ever."

"The people really came. I'm absolutely thrilled." Gabi was also relieved. She hadn't realized how nervous she was about event's success. But when the people started trickling in a little before five, she was able to breathe a little easier. "Thank you for the support, but I didn't do it, this is the result of the whole committee and the community. It was a real *it takes a village* situation."

Danielle laughed. "Well, I'm proud of you, my friend. You did what you set out to do here." Her gaze narrowed. "And what about with Ainsley? Have you decided to put your stubbornness aside? You know, since she's no longer working for Gustare Foods, she won't be moving around all the time, so that excuse is invalid."

"No." Gabi sighed. Her stubbornness had become moot. "She's moving to Florida."

"Florida?"

"To live at her parents' place while she figures out what she's going to do next." Gabi waved at David and Jon as they passed Luca's Bakery tent. "She's leaving tomorrow morning."

"Even after you told her how you feel?" Danielle's eyes clouded with pity.

"I didn't tell her," Gabi confessed. "After she said she was leaving so soon, what was the point?"

"The point is she doesn't know you want her to stay."

Gabi felt hope swelling in her chest. *Hold on, don't get ahead of yourself here.* Hearing Ainsley say she was leaving was hard enough. Laying her feelings on the line and then having Ainsley say she was going to leave nonetheless would be too much. It would break her heart. She shook her head. "No. Her mind is made up. Her career was everything to her, and now it's all messed up. She just wants to hide out at her parents' house and figure it out. In Florida."

Danielle stopped dead in her tracks despite the crowd moving around them. She took Gabi by the shoulders. "You cannot let this woman go without telling her how you feel. I know you, and I know you'll regret it. You'll end up chasing after her and it will be this whole big thing that could have been avoided. She's here now and you're here now, so tell her."

Gabi's stomach twisted. There was a very good reason why she shouldn't do that. "What if she says she doesn't feel the same way?" The question came out in a frightened whisper.

"Gabriella." Danielle's expression brightened. "What if she says she does?"

* * *

With a renewed sense of hope, Gabi made her way to the stage and picnic tables where she had arranged to meet Ainsley for dinner. Danielle was right—she couldn't let this chance pass by. Accordion music played in the background as their eyes met across the sea of tables filled with patrons enjoying pizza and cannoli. Ainsley gave an enthusiastic wave from her spot with the card club gang—an encouraging sign. Gabi's steps quickened as she wove her way between the tables.

After greeting the others at the table, Gabi suggested they take a walk to check out their dinner options. When they'd put a little distance between them and the accordion music, she pulled Ainsley to the side of the crowd. "Before we eat, there's something I need to tell you."

Ainsley nodded. "I wanted to talk to you about something too." She swallowed hard. "But you go first."

Relief. Gabi wasn't sure she could wait any longer anyway. She hadn't exactly planned what she was going to say, but she knew she had to get it out. This was not the kind of anticipation one wanted to savor—it was more of the gut-wrenching, heart-stopping kind.

"Okay," she began. *Words. Say them.* "I know you're planning to leave tomorrow, and you're probably all packed and ready to go because you're the most organized and prepared person I know, but—"

"Gabi, I—"

"No." Gabi held up a halting hand. She needed to get through it before she lost her nerve. "Please, I need to say my thing." *Deep breath.* "I don't want you to leave. I mean, I want you to stay. Here. In Bloomfield."

Ainsley's expression reflected surprise, but not necessarily displeasure, so after another gulp of air, Gabi plunged ahead.

"Please stay. D'Angelo's needs you. No, wait." Gabi squeezed her eyes shut and summoned her courage. If she was going to have any chance of success here, she needed to be completely honest with Ainsley. It was all or nothing. "Please stay. *I'm* the one who needs you. Because I'm falling in love with you. And I know you need to figure out your career, and I'll totally help you. Or I'll give you all the space you need to do it yourself. Whatever you want. Just please stay here."

"You're not upset with me about the whole Linda thing?" Despite the waver in her voice, Ainsley's eyes were hopeful.

"Ainsley, that is all in the past. I'm not interested in the past—Gustare Foods, Linda, all that garbage. I'm interested in the future. Specifically, our future. You and me moving forward together. Please say you'll give us a chance to have that."

Ainsley's plump lips parted as if she was going to respond, but instead she launched herself into Gabi's arms, nearly toppling her over, and kissed her hard and wonderfully right on the mouth.

"Does that mean you'll stay?" Gabi whispered hopefully against Ainsley's lips when they finally came up for air.

A huge smile split Ainsley's face. "Yes."

Gabi's heart drummed, and she let out a yelp of excitement. But then she remembered… "Wait. You said you wanted to talk about something too. What was it?"

Ainsley's face shone, radiant with confidence as she grabbed both of Gabi's hands. "Oddly enough, I wanted to tell you I've decided to stay here in Bloomfield because I kind of love it here, and you and I make a great team. And also, I'm falling in love with you too."

"Then I guess that's settled," Gabi said and before she floated away with the joy that felt like a bunch of balloons filling her chest, she wrapped her arms around Ainsley and kissed her again.

CHAPTER TWENTY-EIGHT

Despite dancing the night away at the festival, then going back to Gabi's for a more private celebration of their pronouncement to one another, Ainsley had slept better than she had since she'd arrived in Bloomfield. Waking up in Gabi's arms, knowing this was only the first of many mornings like it to come put a certain sheen on the break of day. The sun peeking through the edge of the blinds seemed to beckon to them with the promise of fun.

Their morning kiss had made her heart soar. Even the coffee brewing in the kitchen smelled especially heavenly and inviting. Ainsley was filled with all those silly feelings that came with a new love in bloom. They had a busy day at the Slice of Italy ahead of them, but Ainsley was energized and ready to go. It was astounding what a little love could do for a mood.

They arrived at the festival just as it was starting up for the day, but people were already pouring in. Folks milled around in the blocked-off street, and the long line at the specialty coffee truck was a sure sign that people were fueling up for a day of fun.

"It looks like it's going to be another busy day," Ainsley said, giving Gabi's hand a squeeze. They'd been holding hands since they left the house, and even though she knew she'd have to release Gabi eventually so she could tend to her committee duties, she wasn't ready to do so quite yet. "I'm thinking we should beat the crowd and grab a funnel cake for a late breakfast."

"Babe, this is festival eating." Gabi flashed a grin. "We don't even bother naming meals during festival eating. We just graze all day."

Ainsley liked the way the term of endearment rolled off Gabi's tongue. A ripple of excitement worked its way up her spine. Since she'd decided to stay, everything had felt right, like she had found the key to a chest holding priceless treasure. And it was all hers for the taking.

She sniffed the air, catching a whiff of another tantalizing treat that sparked memories of their morning at the Strip District. "In that case, I'm first going to head for the food truck serving chicken on a stick."

Gabi kissed her temple. "You can have whatever you want."

Ainsley pulled Gabi close and slipped her hands into the back pockets of her cut-off jeans. "If that's true, then maybe we should slip behind the wine-tasting tent and have a good old-fashioned make-out session."

"Maybe we should," Gabi murmured against her lips before kissing her again. She tangled her hands in Ainsley's hair and deepened the kiss. Her tongue traced Ainsley's bottom lip before pushing in further.

"Hey, you two." Danielle's cheerful voice interrupted them before things got too hot and heavy. "Let's keep it PG-13 here at the festival."

The kiss dissolved into giggling, and they separated to greet their friend.

Gabi held up her hands in surrender. "Just sharing a smooch with my girlfriend."

Danielle's surprised gaze snapped between Gabi and Ainsley. "You two are...are you really...did you say, *girlfriend*?"

Gabi slung a casual arm around Ainsley's shoulder. "Yes, I did."

"It's official." Ainsley's stomach fluttered with happiness. "We're together and I'm staying in Bloomfield."

"No more Gustare Foods," Gabi added gleefully.

"What are you going to do now?" Danielle asked, but when Ainsley merely shook her head, she suggested, "You should start your own restaurant consulting company. Only, maybe you just help them to improve, and you don't actually take them over in the end." She gave a teasing wink. Apparently word of Gustare Foods' true intentions had gotten around now that the contract had been dissolved and the crisis averted. "Seriously, you're very good at what you do."

It was the first idea for her next step that actually appealed to Ainsley. "Maybe I will." She shrugged. She didn't know what would come next for her, but she felt confident that with Gabi by her side, she would figure it out. Career worries could wait for another day. The only thing on Ainsley's mind that morning was enjoying the festival with her girlfriend.

"Where's Darrius?" Gabi asked. "Is he ready for the big show tonight?"

"He's thrilled. You should see him." Danielle laughed. "All I've heard from him for weeks is how his hero Gabi got him and the band a gig of a lifetime. He really does love Slice of Italy."

"Well, good, 'cause he saved it this year," Gabi said as she tied her hair back with an elastic. The sun was really heating up and apparently she was feeling it.

"Don't be ridiculous." Ainsley bumped their hips. "I'm sure we're all excited to see Sweaty Yeti, but it was you and the committee that made this happen."

"And you too," Gabi reminded her with a sparkle in her eye. "Let's face it, a lot of great things happen when you and I work together."

"I'm glad you feel that way." Ainsley pulled her girlfriend into her arms again. "Because I intend to keep it like that for a very long time.

The noise and chaos of the festival around them dropped away. For that moment, as they stood locked in each other's arms, it was only the two of them, and a future that was open to possibility.

"A *very* long time," Gabi echoed before drawing her in for a kiss.

Whatever was to come next, they'd find it together.

EPILOGUE

One Year Later

Gabi clasped the gold chain around her neck and touched her fingertip to the heart charm, as was her habit, before stepping out of her office at the restaurant. She wished her mother could be there to witness this day. They had closed the restaurant even earlier than normal on a Sunday for the occasion. The quiet in the kitchen felt solemn, but this was a day of celebration. The party was just on the other side of the swinging doors.

Ainsley was waiting for her, playing with the diamond ring on her finger, looking absolutely stunning in a simple lavender wrap dress. But it was the glowing smile on Ainsley's face that made Gabi's belly flutter.

Gabi held up her matching left hand as she walked toward her. "It feels weird to be wearing jewelry in the kitchen, right?" She winked. "You're not going to write me up or something, are you?"

Blue eyes flashing with lust, Ainsley pulled her into her arms. "Believe me, the way you look in those tight jeans, writing you up is not the thing I'm thinking about doing."

"Well, that is not what I planned on surprising our party guests with." Gabi laughed. "Any minute now Pop is going to call us out there to make the announcement."

What a year it had been since Gabi's pop made the announcement about the family restaurant. Back then, neither of them had thought the other would still be at the restaurant. But here they were. Ainsley had decided to stay in Bloomfield, and the women had continued to run D'Angelo's together—Gabi in the kitchen, Ainsley in the dining room. It had turned out to be a magic combination…in so many ways.

Something had shifted in Gabi once she'd had time to process her nonna's sage advice—focus on your actual dream. Her dream was making the food that she loved in the neighborhood that she loved, with the woman she loved by her side. Over the past year, the dream had become her reality.

Ainsley was following her dreams as well. She had started a consulting business on the side, sharing her best-practices checklists along with her wealth of food-code knowledge with restaurants that needed help getting their businesses back on track.

"It's been a great year." Gabi planted a tender kiss on Ainsley's lips. "With many more yet to come, running our family business together."

"I love being part of your family," Ainsley murmured against her lips before pulling her in for another, more passionate kiss.

Gabi's heart pounded as she tangled her hands in Ainsley's hair, letting the thrill of the moment wash over her. How had she gotten so damned lucky? She could kiss this woman every day for the rest of her life, and that was exactly what she planned on doing.

"Hey, you two." Danielle's stage whisper from the swinging doors of the dining room broke the spell. "It's time."

As they broke off the kiss, Gabi took Ainsley's hand, giving it a squeeze as they followed Danielle.

"Here they are!" Pop's voice boomed as they joined him on the makeshift stage in the dining room. "I'm so pleased to announce to you that my daughter, Gabi, and Ainsley, who you all know and love, are engaged to be married!"

The crowd of friends and family who had gathered to celebrate them burst out in applause punctuated by congratulatory hoots and hollers.

Through teary eyes, Gabi looked out at the sea of faces. Everyone looked so happy for them—Nonna, Brian, Jane, Uncle Sal and Mary Louise, even Ruby and the card club among so many other dear friends. It felt like the whole community had shown up for them.

When the crowd finally began to settle down, Nonna called out, "Kiss! Kiss!" getting them all riled up again.

"I have to listen to my nonna," Gabi said with a shrug as she faced her fiancée. "Besides, I love you, Ainsley Becker."

"I love you, Gabriella D'Angelo."

And in front of all their friends and family, in the restaurant they happily ran together, they sealed their promise to one another with a kiss.

Bella Books, Inc.
Women. Books. Even Better Together.
P.O. Box 10543
Tallahassee, FL 32302
Phone: (800) 729-4992
www.BellaBooks.com

More Titles from Bella Books

Hunter's Revenge – Gerri Hill
978-1-64247-447-3 | 276 pgs | paperback: $18.95 | eBook: $9.99
Tori Hunter is back! Don't miss this final chapter in the acclaimed Tori Hunter series.

Integrity – E. J. Noyes
978-1-64247-465-7 | 28 pgs | paperback: $19.95 | eBook: $9.99
It was supposed to be an ordinary workday...

The Order – TJ O'Shea
978-1-64247-378-0 | 396 pgs | paperback: $19.95 | eBook: $9.99
For two women the battle between new love and old loyalty may prove more dangerous than the war they're trying to survive.

Under the Stars with You – Jaime Clevenger
978-1-64247-439-8 | 302 pgs | paperback: $19.95 | eBook: $9.99
Sometimes believing in love is the first step. And sometimes it's all about trusting the stars.

The Missing Piece – Kat Jackson
978-1-64247-445-9 | 250 pgs | paperback: $18.95 | eBook: $9.99
Renee's world collides with possibility and the past, setting off a tidal wave of changes she could have never predicted.

An Acquired Taste – Cheri Ritz
978-1-64247-462-6 | 206 pgs | paperback: $17.95 | eBook: $9.99
Can Elle and Ashley stand the heat in the *Celebrity Cook Off* kitchen?

Printed in the USA
CPSIA information can be obtained
at www.ICGtesting.com
JSHW020315070624
64403JS00008B/3